Champagne and Bullets

Military Moguls

Book One

Olivia Jaymes

www.OliviaJaymes.com

CHAMPAGNE AND BULLETS
Print Edition
Copyright © 2015 by Olivia Jaymes

Dedication

To all the servicemen and women who leave behind loved ones to serve their country.

Champagne and Bullets

Almost fourteen years ago Sebastian Gibbs and Amanda Rosemont called off their society wedding after a huge argument. She accused him of being too controlling and he accused her of being too immature. Neither were all that wrong.

Amanda has rebuilt her life since Seb left and has done a pretty damn good job of it. Great friends, her own business, and a peaceful life. She hardly ever thinks about him anymore.

Hired by Seb's mother to plan a party for him, Amanda is thrown back into his life. She's determined to keep her distance but just seeing him again shakes her to the core. It's not going to be easy to hold herself together for this job.

Seb never stopped loving Amanda. When he'd left he thought he was doing the right thing. But one look at her and he knows there isn't anything he won't do to win her back. Is it too late for a second chance at true love?

Chapter One

SEBASTIAN GIBBS HAD never been able to convince his mother of anything. Not when he was five and wanted to keep the dog that had wandered into their yard. Not later when he was ten and wanted to raise exotic spiders and snakes. Not even when he was seventeen and was trying to get her to believe that he hadn't thrown a beer bash while she and his father were out of town one weekend.

Lucinda Eleanor Montgomery Gibbs was very much like all her forebearers in the Montgomery dynasty. Relentless. When she wanted something to be a certain way she made sure it happened. End of story. Today she wanted Seb to do the very last thing in the world he wanted to do.

"I don't think it's a good idea, Mother."

Seb cradled the phone between his cheek and shoulder and leaned back in the soft leather chair, propping his feet up on the dark oak desk and rubbing at the ache in his thigh. After being shot in the leg several years ago in Kabul he could predict the weather by how much it hurt. It was going to storm like a son of a bitch by all indications, but then it was summer in Florida and that was pretty much a daily occurrence.

He needed to get this call over with so he could resume the tedious but necessary job of setting up his new office. As it stood at the moment, the room was overflowing with boxes and the walls bare. At his uncle's uptown law firm there would have been an assistant to take care of this. But Seb had no desire to join that firm or be that variety of attorney.

"From the time you were a little boy you haven't liked anyone's ideas but your own. I'm asking you for a favor, Seb, and you haven't given me one good reason not to do it."

Reining in his frustration, he reminded himself that his mother wasn't aware of his feelings regarding this particular favor. In fact, he'd taken great pains to make sure no one was aware of them, except Dane and Christian, of course.

"I just don't think it's a good idea for me to see Amanda. There's a lot of water under that bridge. I doubt she wants to see me as well. We didn't part on the best of terms."

"She must have put it all behind her because she's agreed to take on the job of planning your firm's opening party. She's going to stop by your office this afternoon and talk to you about it. You can discuss the case with her while she's there."

Seb swung his legs down and sat up straight, every nerve in his body at attention. He must have misheard his mother. It sounded like Amanda was coming to the office to talk to him. Today. They hadn't spoken in almost thirteen years.

"I don't want to see Amanda, Mother." His tone was sharp but he couldn't let this happen. He'd been able to keep his life together all these years by not revisiting the past.

His mother gave him a long-suffering sigh. "I want to throw this party for your new law firm. I'm proud of you. Why are you being so difficult?"

"I am not being difficult." Seb's teeth were gnashed together. "I am being realistic. Why is Amanda planning this party anyway?"

"She's started her own event business. Since the divorce she's been involved in various charities but wanted to have something of her own. I'm happy to support her efforts."

As if Amanda Rosemont needed the money. Her family had been walking in tall cotton for several generations. The event planning was probably something to keep her from being a bored socialite. She'd always been full of more energy than she could burn.

"Fine. Why don't you throw Gerard a birthday party instead? He loves shit like that."

"Your brother would be more grateful, and watch your language. I'm still your mother. Now I have an appointment, so simply promise me that you will meet with Amanda. She'll have questions about your preferences for the party and then the two of you can discuss the legal matter she needs help with." Seb rubbed his forehead where a headache was starting to form. "Are you still there, Seb?"

"I'm here." Seb loved his mother too much not to give in to what she wanted. Sometimes he wished he could be more like Dane Braxton, one of his two best friends. Dane couldn't stand his family and rarely spent any time with them. Seb, on the other hand adored his parents, especially his mother. He'd known all along that he would give her whatever she wanted. He'd only been delaying the inevitable. "Of course I'll meet with Amanda if that's what you need me to do."

"Thank you." Lucinda Gibbs' voice didn't sound so much triumphant as pleased and loving.

She had no idea what this seemingly innocuous meeting was going to cost him.

Not in dollars, but in peace of mind.

Seb chatted with his mother for a few more minutes before hanging up. Tossing the cell phone down on the desk, he stood to look out the office windows. There wasn't much to see except for the cheesy man-made lake in the business complex where they'd rented space. The dream of opening this law firm had been thirteen years in the making but it was finally happening.

"I'm running out for some lunch. If you want something, now is the time to place your order."

Christian Rhodes, the third partner and other best friend, stood in the doorway with a grin, his car keys dangling from his fingers.

Seb cleared his throat but couldn't clear the picture of Amanda that had taken up residence in his brain. Had she changed much? Was her blonde hair still as shiny and golden? Did her light blue eyes still sparkle with life and mischief? "I could eat. Where are you headed?"

"I was going to grab some takeout from the sports bar down the road." Chris tilted his head as he surveyed Seb. "But I could be persuaded to eat in. Maybe get a beer. You look like you could use one."

Seb wasn't one to talk about his feelings, but this was Chris. There were no two people Seb was closer to on this planet than Chris and Dane. They'd grown up together, friends since before kindergarten.

"Amanda is coming here this afternoon."

Letting the words hang in the air between them, Chris's eyes grew wide and he shook his head.

"Shit. Let's make that two beers. I'll get Dane. What is she coming here for anyway?"

Rubbing the back of his neck, Sebastian pointed to his cell. "Mother called. Amanda is planning the party for our opening. She also needs to talk to me about some legal issue from one of the charities she works with. I tried to get out of it but you know what my mom is like."

Chris nodded in sympathy. "A veritable steamroller. Can you handle this?"

"I can't avoid Amanda forever, although I've been trying to this last year since I moved back. We have too many friends and family in common. This was bound to happen. At least I have a warning."

Chris looked like he didn't know what to say, and Seb didn't know what else to say either. It was a cluster of massive proportions.

"Why does everyone look like they're headed to a funeral?" Dane appeared in the doorway and slapped Chris on the back. "I thought you were going to get some lunch. I'm starved."

Seb simply shook his head and leaned against his desk. Poor Dane had no idea what he'd walked into.

Finally Chris spoke. "Amanda is coming here this afternoon to see Seb."

The smile on Dane's face disappeared and his shoulders stiffened. "Why?"

"Relax, bro. Mother asked her to plan the party for our opening plus listen to some legal issue she's got. It will be fine." Seb actually sounded like he believed it.

"She can meet with me." Dane stuck out his chin as if taking a punch for Seb. "You don't need to deal with this shit."

Seb's friend was overprotective and stubborn as all hell. Heaven help the woman he ended up with.

"It's time," Seb said quietly. "I need to face this."

"We'll do whatever you want," Chris assured him. "We can meet with her or you can. It's up to you."

"I'll meet with her but first I really do need that beer. Is the offer still open?" Seb scooped up his phone and keys.

"It is. Let's go." Chris led the way, followed by Dane and Seb. He still had some time before Amanda showed up at the office. Before the past came barreling back into the present. It was time to man up and face the only woman he'd ever loved.

The woman he'd planned to marry and make a life with, but somehow things had gone awry. Now he was still single and Amanda was divorced.

And no matter how much he might still love her, there wasn't going to be a second chance for him. For them.

Chapter Two

AMANDA SHOULDN'T HAVE taken this job. She'd allowed Lucinda Gibbs to talk her into something that could only end in more pain and she'd had enough of that to last her a lifetime.

It had been almost thirteen years since Amanda had seen Seb. She could still remember the day they'd called off their impending nuptials because of an argument that had flown out of control. They'd ripped each other's hearts into tiny pieces over stupid little things that looking back hadn't really mattered. But she'd been young, only twenty, and at that age everything mattered. Too much.

They'd argued in the months leading up to the wedding. About him joining the Army. About where she'd live while he was gone. About her education and his as well. About all sorts of things that seemed so important at the time. They'd been too damn young to have any clue what they were doing, although Seb had been twenty-five and had just graduated from law school.

If she were honest? Both their lives had been far too easy up until that point. They'd never had to struggle for anything, their family money and connections smoothing the path. Neither one had been ready for the work and compromise of marriage and a lifetime commitment.

Not long after they'd called it off he'd left for the Army, clearly done with her and their relationship. No letters. No emails. No phone calls. She'd been in love with Seb since she was fourteen years old and suddenly it was over. She'd had no choice but to move on. He wasn't coming back. It didn't matter that she'd regretted the things she'd said to him. She was sure he hadn't meant them either.

They'd simply been young, dumb, and stubborn.

Standing in front of the door to his new law firm she smoothed down the skirt of her white business suit and took a deep, calming breath. She was a grown woman now, married and divorced. Seeing him would be a shock to her system but perhaps it was for the best. Now that he was back in the Tampa area, they were bound to run into one another eventually.

Tucking her purse under her arm, she opened the door and walked into the office. Obviously still a work in progress, there were boxes everywhere and no one in sight. The reception desk was bare and she took a few tentative steps forward to peek around the open doorway and down a hall.

"Hello?" The office door at the end was open and she headed toward it, hoping she hadn't called when no one was here. "Is anyone in?"

"I'm here, Amanda." Seb's deep voice came from down the hall. Memories so vivid she could almost feel and taste them came rushing back, sucking the air from her lungs and making her stomach twist into knots. She didn't want to feel anything for him. But all her brain seemed to remember at the moment were the good things. There had been so many of those.

Ruthlessly pushing her emotions away, she straightened up and marched down the hall until she was looking into the whiskey-brown eyes of Sebastian Gibbs. Her knees felt like jelly but she determinedly lifted her chin and straightened her shoulders. It was show time. She would not allow her inner turmoil to be displayed. Later when she was alone she could fall apart.

"Seb. It's good to see you." Her voice had come out huskier than she'd planned but he might not notice. He looked the same but different too. His hair was that inimitable golden blond but now she could see a few gray hairs at his temples. His skin was just as tanned but now there were lines around his eyes and mouth. Typical for men, they didn't detract from his good looks in the least, simply making him look more mature and distinguished than that last day. Amanda had no such hope that time had been as kind to her. "I hope this isn't a bad time to stop in."

"Of course not. We're not really open as you can see, but I always have time for an old friend."

An old friend? The words shoved a dagger into her already bleeding heart. At one time she'd planned to have this man's children and grow old with him. Had dedicated her life to making him happy. Now he'd relegated her to friendship status.

Seb indicated one of the chairs at the small round conference table on one side of his office and Amanda sank down into it gratefully. Pulling a file folder and a pen from her handbag, she wanted to get this meeting over as soon as possible, unsure how long she could keep this calm facade in place.

He settled in the other chair only about a foot away. Too near—she could smell the familiar scent of his aftershave and feel the heat from his body. She'd come too far to allow him to affect her in this way, but her senses had immediately come to life the moment she'd laid eyes on him. Visions of the past she'd never been able to bury. He'd spoiled her for any other lover.

Fidgeting in her chair, Amanda clicked the pen open and pulled out a stack of papers from the folder.

"I'm sure you're busy, so let's get started." Tapping her pen nervously, she gazed unseeingly at the forms in front of her. "Your mother gave me some information but I'll need to confirm it. How many people are you expecting at the party?"

"About a hundred or so. We sent out a hundred and seventy-five invitations but we've only heard from about half."

Frowning, she glanced around the office. "Do you have more space than what I've seen?"

"The party won't be held here." Seb sat up straighter and shook his head. "It's being held at my home in Wesley Chapel. They finished the construction three months ago. There's plenty of room there."

Her heart lurched at the thought that he had perhaps built a home for a woman that he loved. Amanda and Seb had spent so many hours planning their life together and their dream house had been so real in her mind.

"Fine. I'll just need the address." Seb rattled it off and she scratched it down before turning to the rest of the questions. They moved through each one easily but the tension between them continued to grow. By the time she was finished it was nearly unbearable. "I'll get a plan and a quote put together and email it to you."

She tucked the forms back in the folder and took a steadying breath. A big part of her wanted to run out the front door now that they had finished the first part of her business, but her sense of responsibility wouldn't let her bolt. She needed his legal help badly.

"Mother said you had a legal problem."

Amanda had been staring at the papers since she sat down but now she couldn't avoid looking into his eyes.

"I do." She recrossed her legs restlessly, not sure how to begin. "For several years I've been volunteering at a battered women's shelter in the area. It's located in one of those old large Victorians in St. Pete. It's a quiet and very secret location for obvious reasons. We don't want the spouses showing up there causing trouble."

"Have you been having issues?" Seb stroked his chin, his expression thoughtful. "I know some people that could put in a state of the art security system."

"We have one of those—that's not our problem. It's not the spouses that are the issue. It's a developer. He wants to buy up all the houses in that area and turn them into condos or something. He and his people have been harassing our residents and the neighbors. He's managed to buy up several homes but he wants the entire block."

Seb's eyebrow quirked up. "As my grandfather always said, it's good to want things. Doesn't mean you get them, though. Is he offering market?"

"Slightly below. The shelter is run by a foundation, and by the time it paid the broker's fees, the movers and everything else, it would take a net loss on the sale. It put a great deal of money into a renovation. The shelter has only been there for eighteen months, not nearly long enough to build up any kind of equity, either."

"And you want me to do what, exactly?"

Impatience made her want to kick Seb in the shins. He'd always been like this, thoughtful in word and deed. He didn't do things lightly, always weighing the pros and cons. He'd been the perfect balance to her full speed ahead attitude.

"I want you to scare the developer. Just a little," she huffed. "I want him to know that we're not some two-bit outfit that can be run off with some intimidation tactics. That we have muscle."

For the first time in thirteen years Amanda watched a smile cross Seb's face, rendering her momentarily speechless. It made him look twenty-five again and she was taken back to 2001.

"And I'm that muscle?" Seb chuckled and stood, going to lean on the desk. Crossing his arms over his wide chest, he looked more amused than anything. Was he going to help her or not?

"I know you can be intimidating and forceful." Did she ever. Seb in the bedroom was a dominant force of sensuality she'd never gotten over. "Are you on the developer's side? Are you one of those people that think we're standing in the way of progress?"

"No, I am not," he replied smoothly. "I'm not any more fond of those cookie cutter condo developments than most people. However, if he offers a fair price, then who am I to say what should be built?"

"But he's not," she protested, "He offered below market."

"What if I speak with him and he makes a new offer? What if it's generous? Are you willing to entertain it?" Seb leaned forward, his palms flat on the desk. "I need to know what you really want me to do, Mandy. If you just want me to scare him, that's fine. If you want me to get a better offer, I can do that too."

Her entire body stiffened and a bolt of electricity shot through her spine. Seb was the only person in the world that called her Mandy, and she hadn't heard it from his lips in thirteen years. Hearing it again brought too many memories rushing back and she had to take a few breaths to control the pain taking root in her heart.

"We'd have to sell at a premium to make it worth our while," Amanda answered stiffly. "We would of course look at any fair offer, but first he needs to promise to stop harassing people."

"I'll talk to him then, but it won't be today."

Seb straightened from where he was leaning on the desk and she stood as well. She needed to get out of here. As she had feared, seeing Seb hadn't been a good idea. All it had done was resurrect a past that she'd spent years trying to bury.

She reached into her purse and pulled out a business card. "This is the contact information he gave us. I appreciate your help on this."

Seb's fingers briefly brushed her own as he took the card from her hand. The skin tingled and burned where they had touched and Amanda snatched her hand back as if an actual flame had licked at the flesh. Tucking her arm behind her, she tried to compose her features so he wouldn't see how he affected her all these years later. It was pathetic how she was allowing this to happen.

"I'll be in touch after I talk to him."

Seb placed the card on his desk as she backed toward the door. The urge to flee was strong and if she stayed here much longer she was going to do something she would later regret. She checked her watch as if she had a pressing appointment.

"I need to fly. Thank you, Seb."

Amanda fumbled with her keys and sunglasses, not realizing Seb had moved from his spot behind the desk. Before she was able to strengthen her defenses he was standing right next to her, a smile on his gorgeous face.

"It was good seeing you, Mandy."

She shoved her sunglasses over her eyes before he could see them bright with tears. "It was good seeing you too, Seb. Take care."

Somehow she managed to walk out of the office and to her car, the oppressive Florida heat and humidity wrapping around her immediately. Starting the engine, she flicked the air conditioner on high until the cool air was blowing her hair back and drying the sweat that had gathered at the nape of her neck. A stray tear fell down her cheek and she brushed it away with a trembling hand.

She'd already cried too many tears in her life. They didn't change a thing.

Chapter Three

SEB AND CHRISTIAN sat down at the back of the bar where it was slightly more quiet. It had been another long day at the office, although this one had seemed to drag on more than normal as practically everything seemed to remind him of Amanda.

She'd looked so damn beautiful.

Like a vision of summer with her golden hair and cornflower blue eyes, she didn't look a day older than when he'd last seen her. But there had been a strong, silent maturity that was new. This Amanda wouldn't tolerate any of his shenanigans or alpha male macho crap.

"You don't have to do this, you know." Christian nodded his thanks to the waitress as she took their order.

"I do. I promised Mom." Even to Seb's own ears it sounded like a lame-ass excuse.

"The fact that this is for Amanda has nothing to do with it?" Christian persisted. "Don't even try to lie to me."

"You know how I feel about her." Seb sure as hell didn't want to discuss it. Seeing Amanda yesterday after all these years had changed everything. All that he thought was in the past had been resurrected. He'd barely slept last night as thoughts of her haunted him, making sleep impossible.

"What are you going to do about it?"

"I think I forfeited the right to do anything about it when I acted like an ass thirteen years ago. I was trying to run her life when I could barely manage my own. I can't imagine she's forgotten that." His words came out more bitter than he'd planned.

"Would you still try and do that? I doubt it. You've changed and I'm betting she has too. Maybe then it wasn't the right time but now might be a different story."

The waitress slid two beers in front of them with a smile before bustling to the next table.

"Amanda was twenty years old. So fucking young—not that I was much older at twenty-five. God, I was so arrogant. I thought I had all the answers to life. I didn't have shit."

"We all thought that we did but some never

realize they don't. At least you've admitted your part in all this. Perhaps if you just talked to her, told her you've changed."

"And then she'll throw her arms around me and tell me all is forgiven." Seb snorted in derision. "It will be like the past never happened."

"It happened alright," Christian shot back. "But she's a grown woman now and I think she can handle you."

"Drop it." Seb took a long drink of his beer. He loved Christian like a brother but going over and over the past wasn't going to change a damn thing. Seb had ruined the best thing he'd ever had. He'd long ago realized he wasn't going to get some magical second chance. Life didn't work that way.

"For now," Christian conceded. "So tell me about this real estate thing she has you working on. Do you need any help?"

"That's why you're here. I figured two lawyers would be more intimidating than one. And if things go downhill, you can keep me from taking a swing at him if he says anything derogatory about dealing with Mandy."

"You're assuming I won't want to punch him myself," Christian laughed. "Is that your guy?" He jerked his thumb at a medium-height man with dark, slicked-back hair, and a slight paunch that was still visible despite his blue business suit. Seb nodded and waved his hand in the air to get the man's attention. He recognized Lance from the picture on his business card.

Seb and Christian shook hands with Lance as he joined them at the table. Christian signaled to the waitress who came over to get Lance's order.

"Thanks for meeting with me." Seb wanted to get this over and done with so he didn't waste any time. "I'd like to talk to you about a property you're trying to purchase. The women's shelter?"

"Ah yes, the shelter. Good piece of land and a solid resale value neighborhood. Plus there are stores nearby and quick access to main roads. The school district is up and coming to boot." Seb ignored the fifteen-second commercial even as the waitress brought Lance's iced tea. "Sorry I can't join you in a beer but I have some clients to meet with after this. Real estate is twenty-four-seven, you know."

Seb cleared this throat and leaned forward. "I'm speaking with you today purely off the record. Professional to professional, if you will."

The man grinned and nodded. "Man to man, eh? I can appreciate that. It's just as well to keep the girls out of this. I've found females to be way too emotional during negotiations. Ms. Rosemont seems to have a certain attachment to that house that could blind her to the benefits of selling."

What a misogynistic jerk. No wonder Amanda didn't want to deal with him. He needed to be taken down a peg or two.

Ignoring Lance's opinion of females in general, Seb continued. "Negotiations are one thing, but harassment is something else. I won't tolerate you showing up at the house unannounced and uninvited. If you have something to say, then you say it to me."

He kept his tone calm but firm and Lance's friendly visage seemed to disappear within seconds. Seb had obviously hit a nerve. Amanda hadn't been exaggerating.

Lance patted his mouth with a paper napkin before he spoke. "I take it that you are now representing Ms. Rosement?"

"*We* are representing Ms. Rosement," Christian interjected. "And unless you have a better offer than *below market*, there really isn't anything left to say."

Lance's face went red and he slammed down the napkin. "That was a fair offer. That woman has an inflated sense of what the market will bear."

"It was a lousy offer," Seb said flatly. "I checked the comps. You low-balled the offer and you know it. My colleague is correct. Unless you have a better offer we don't have anything else to discuss."

Lance stood and dug angrily into his pocket but Seb shook his head. "Your tea is on us."

"Fine." The man balled up the napkin and tossed it on the table. "It's a good offer and your client should take it."

"Let me know if you have a better one." This time Seb stood and held out his business card, wanting to make sure his point was driven home. "Until then, this discussion is over."

"Gladly," Lance huffed before shoving Seb's card in his pocket and striding out of the bar. Seb sat back down and took a drink from his beer as Christian eyed him from over the rim of his glass.

Chris whistled and grinned. "I didn't realize you had done that much research regarding the property values. Very well done."

Seb chuckled and signaled for the waitress. "I didn't do shit, actually. But I can see this guy is slimy. He gives honest real estate developers a bad name. I took a shot and it paid off. Besides, Amanda has never been one for drama. If she says he's been harassing people and he offered less than market, then he did. Period."

"Maybe she's changed?" Christian countered.

"People do, you know."

"Not about this." Seb shook his head, knowing who she was deep down was still the same. The waitress came up to their table and Seb ordered a platter of wings and another round of beers.

"Then maybe how she feels about you hasn't changed either."

Seb didn't even bother to respond and he was pretty sure Christian didn't expect one. There was no point going around and around about Amanda. The only thing he could do was live in the present and try not to think too much about his empty future.

Chapter Four

"I CAN'T BELIEVE I let you talk me into this." Amanda's fingers tightened nervously on the delicate crystal flute as she sipped the bubbling champagne. "I could run into him here."

"Here" was a lavish party being thrown by the Welchel family in their rambling beachside mansion. Rich fabrics, marble floors, and an intricate chandelier highlighted a decor that screamed conspicuous consumption.

They had obviously spared no expense in either food, booze, or decorations. The large ballroom that spilled onto a balcony overlooking the Gulf of Mexico sparkled with beautiful people bedecked in satin, silk, and diamonds. While the home was lovely, Amanda preferred the view from the terrace where she could listen to the waves and smell the salt air.

"You're not going to run into Emmett. Didn't

you say he's living in New York?" Darby Spellman asked. Darby was one of Amanda's best friends from way back. With golden brown hair and dark blue eyes, he was handsome, smart, and charming. Amanda loved Darby like a brother, not a lover though. They'd kissed once when they were both thirteen and realized they were destined to be friends only. But that didn't mean he wouldn't drag her out of the house on occasion to play his date for the evening, and tonight was one of those nights.

"Emmett is living in New York. In a Fifth Avenue apartment my trust fund paid for. But he does come back to visit his family and he's very close to the Welchels. I can imagine him flying in for the party. The last thing I want is to see him. He was livid last time I talked to him."

Emmett Bardner was a sometime financier and full-time asshole. He was also her ex-husband—emphasis on the "ex". She'd been young and on the rebound when she'd met him. He'd been handsome, smooth, and a great actor. After they'd married, he'd laid it on the line that he wasn't planning on working for a living. He'd already burned through his own inheritance so he started in on hers. Five years later she'd divorced him. He had been an expensive mistake, but she did learn.

Darby chuckled, clearly delighted at the thought of Emmett being angry. They'd never got along, taking an instant dislike to one another that had placed Amanda firmly in the middle. But then Darby wasn't a man that made male friends easily, preferring the spotlight for himself.

"That's what happens when he makes a grab for more of your family's money and gets his hand slapped. He must be desperate."

Amanda didn't want to think about Emmett. "I doubt it. He remarried money and his parents still fund him as well from time to time. No, he simply wants to make life difficult for me. I had the nerve to divorce him and he's never going to let me live in peace."

"He's just a nasty piece of work," Darby declared. "You're well rid of him. When I think about how you were when you came back from London–"

"Let's not talk about it," she interrupted, placing her fingers over Darby's lips and shaking her head. Bad memories. "It's in the past. Let it lie there."

"It's not in the past apparently. You let it interfere with your life now."

"I'm not going to discuss this with you, Darby." Amanda sipped at the golden liquid and looked out over the crowded room. "I don't know who did the event but they did a very nice job."

Darby laughed and grabbed another glass of champagne from a passing waiter. "Says the girl who runs her own party planning business. Are you mad that they didn't ask you to do it?"

"I don't think most people take my 'little business' as my parents call it very seriously. They think I'm bored," Amanda sighed.

"Only boring people are bored," Darby declared outrageously. "And baby, you are not boring. Maddening, yes. Stubborn, yes. Boring, no."

"Pot calling the kettle black."

The orchestra struck up a new song and Darby tugged at her hand. "Let's dance, you wild woman. I long to feel you in my arms."

"Liar. You long to feel that cute waitress in your arms."

"True, but right now I'm with you."

Laughing at his exuberance, she let Darby set their glasses on a table and then lead her out onto the dance floor. Full of natural rhythm, he moved to the music easily and Amanda found to her surprise that she was having fun. She hadn't wanted to come tonight, her mind and body exhausted from not sleeping. Since seeing Seb a few days ago, every time she closed her eyes she was tortured with visions of the past. It made for a long, lonely night.

"You can talk to me, sweets. You know that, right?"

Darby's puppy dog eyes were looking down on her, full of sympathy. She shook her head, knowing what he was talking about. He knew she'd met with Seb.

"There's nothing to talk about. I saw him and I'm fine. End of story."

"Are you sure?" Darby's expression was clearly one of disbelief.

"I'm sure." Maybe if she kept saying it she'd actually start believing it. "Everything is okay. Nothing happened."

"That's good, sweets, because Sebastian is here and heading right for us."

Darby had somehow navigated them to the edge of the dance floor and she could clearly see Seb striding toward them. His blond good looks were striking against his all black tuxedo, right down to the shirt and tie. Her heart thumped in her chest and her stomach did somersaults in her abdomen as he moved closer. By the time he tapped Darby on the shoulder she was a mess inside and praying it didn't show.

"May I cut in?"

That voice. It never ceased to stir her arousal. She remembered as if it was yesterday how he would take command of her body with only a few words. It hadn't mattered what he said, really—it had been the timbre, so deep and dark.

"Of course." Darby stepped back with a wink and a smile and Seb took his place, his fingers tangling with hers and his palm at the base of her spine. "I'll find you later, sweets."

Her knees had turned to jelly at his touch and she had to concentrate so she wouldn't step on his toes. They didn't speak but she could smell his aftershave and feel the heat from his body. A deep longing swept over her, almost painful in its strength. This wasn't fair or right. She had moved on, dammit. She had buried the past and now he was digging up the graveyard.

She couldn't let this happen.

As the last notes of the song were played she tried to pull away but his arm didn't budge from where it was wrapped around her waist. She looked up into his brown eyes and the all too familiar passion was still there. She'd recognize that expression anywhere and it shook her to her very core. Nothing had changed. At least physically. She wanted him and he wanted her.

"I need to find Darby." Her voice sounded strange to her own ears.

"Not yet," he cajoled with a charming smile. "One more dance."

"I don't think it's a good idea."

"Are you afraid?" he asked lightly. "I don't bite."

"You do bite, and I am afraid."

SEB DIDN'T WANT her to be afraid of him.

"I don't bite much," he replied finally. "Let's dance."

He'd walked into the party tonight reluctantly, wanting to be anywhere but here. He'd had a long day at the office, and a pizza and some television had sounded better than putting on a tux and pretending to be having fun. But as he'd scanned the crowd his gaze had immediately zeroed in on Amanda. She'd stand out anywhere but tonight she practically shimmered under the soft lights.

Dressed in a long black strapless gown that hugged her curves and pushed up her perfect breasts, she'd been dancing with Darby Spellman. Each time they'd move Seb would catch a glimpse of her tanned leg through the long split in the skirt. She'd been looking up at Darby smiling, her hair pulled back and up so Seb could see the sensuous curve of her neck. Unlike most of the other women at the party, Amanda wore very little jewelry – just a pair of small diamond earrings and a pendant. She didn't need to gild herself—she was naturally alluring.

Emotion had burst wide open inside of him and he'd been powerless to stop himself from walking across the room. She hadn't been able to hide her trepidation at his arrival but he couldn't be sorry he was here. Every cell of his body wanted to be close to her. Talk to her. Touch her.

She seemed to melt into his arms as the music played. Their bodies brushed with each step and his cock began to ache as it pressed against his zipper. Images flashed before his eyes of the two of them, naked and sweaty. Amanda bound to the bed or bent over for his pleasure. Her pussy hot and tight around his cock. Her lips and tongue teasing his dick and balls. No one had turned him on the way her innocent seduction had.

They danced silently, Seb unwilling to disturb the peace between them at this moment. The tension had dissipated only to be replaced with an awareness he couldn't shake. His senses were taking in every detail – her sensual scent, the satin of her skin that seemed to glow under the lights.

He could hear and feel each of her breaths and watch the pulse that beat frantically at the base of her throat. She was just as affected by their nearness as he was. It was more than he'd ever expected and more than he deserved.

The song ended and Amanda backed away, almost knocking over a waitress with a tray of drinks. She apologized to the young woman before nervously looking around the room. Hoping for Darby to come to her rescue? Wasn't going to happen. Taller than Amanda by nearly a foot, Seb had seen Darby chatting up a pretty young thing near the buffet table.

"I think I need some air," she pronounced. "It was good to see you, Seb."

"I'll join you." He slid his hand under her elbow and directed her toward the open balcony. She tried to tug her arm away but he simply wrapped his hand more firmly around the warm flesh and used his other arm to keep her from being jostled in the crowd.

"There's no need," she protested, her eyes wide with alarm. He could feel her body trembling under his fingers and he had to suppress the urge to place her own hand on his heart so she could feel it galloping in his chest.

"It's no bother," he said, deliberately misunderstanding. Being this close to her was complete and utter madness, but he couldn't drag himself away. Like a moth drawn to the flame, he knew he would be burnt. "I could use some fresh air myself."

Leading her to a secluded area behind several plants with oversized leaves, they leaned against the railing. The sound of the water lapping at the shore calmed his overheated senses.

"It's beautiful, isn't it?"

Amanda had never been good with long empty spaces without speaking. Her voice was soft but still clearly audible as she gazed out toward the horizon. A full moon hung over the Gulf, illuminating the beach and painting the waves silver while shadows danced and skipped over the water.

He straightened and drew her toward the stairs to the sand below. At first she hesitated, but then capitulated. The warm night must have been calling to her as much as it was to him.

They kicked off their shoes and left them at the bottom of the stairs. He slipped his hand into hers while his feet sunk into the sand. Her giggle made his heart ache as the cool water tickled her toes and then retreated, only to come back and make her giggle again.

"I don't remember the last time I walked on

the beach."

The wind had loosened her hair from its confining style and tendrils were clinging to her cheeks. He reached out before she could protest or argue, tucking one of them behind her ear.

"We used to come here as often as we could. Remember the time the waves were breaking right before that storm came through?"

"I remember that we got run off by some cops that day," she laughed. "We weren't supposed to be out in that bad weather. We must have been crazy."

"I wanted to surf. We don't get many waves on this side of the state, you know."

"It wasn't the smartest thing we've ever done. Do you still surf?"

"Actually, I do. Dane, Christian, and I went to Hawaii last year and surfed the North Shore. It was the trip of a lifetime."

He didn't mention it was the first trip he'd taken after leaving the Army.

"I've never been there. Not yet, anyway."

Amanda studiously avoided looking at him, instead staring up at the sky. The past was a dangerous thing to talk about. Better to keep things to now.

"Has that Poplin guy been bothering you lately?"

"Not at all. Thank you for talking to him for me. Our regular law firm would have charged me four hundred dollars an hour to do that."

No wonder his mother had pressed him into service. A charitable organization shouldn't be paying crazy fees like that.

"I was happy to help, Mandy. Let me know if I can do anything else."

There was a long silence and finally she turned to look at him, her expression conflicted. The playful, happy moment they'd shared had quickly disappeared. "Please don't."

There was a plea in her voice that pulled at his gut. He'd never been able to turn her down when she sounded that way.

"Don't what? Don't help?"

"Don't call me Mandy." She shook her head and took a few steps back. "I'm not Mandy anymore."

"Funny, you look like Mandy and you sound like her too." He tilted his head and gave her a smile, trying to get back those few seconds of easiness between them. "I don't think you've left her as far behind as you think. You came out here to play on the beach with me, didn't you?"

She turned her back to him, her shoulders rigid. "Just don't call me that. Mandy was a child and I'm a woman."

A beautiful and desirable one. His fingers itched to pull the pins from her hair and then run his hands over her soft curves before pressing her to her knees in the soft sand.

"I don't want to upset you."

Whirling around, she lifted her chin in defiance. "I'm not upset. What I am is leaving. There's no point to any of this. Good night, Seb. It was nice to see you again."

She marched through the soft sand and up to the house, not sparing him even a glance over her shoulder. He'd fucked everything up again. He should have known better than to dance and then spirit her away without clearing the air first.

But one thing was clear to Seb now. He still loved Amanda, and she still had some feelings left for him. Yes, there was anger and hurt there as well. He would have to deal with those but perhaps they could move past all that had happened and build something new.

After seeing her again, he simply could not imagine his life without her in it. He'd been only half-living since he'd left. It was the first time in a long while that he felt awake. Something inside of him had shifted and he couldn't go back to the way things had been.

She might tell him to go to hell, but honestly that's where he'd been already. He had to take this chance and try to reach out to her again. He had to try and win her love.

With more stalwart determination, he marched through the cool sand, retrieving his shoes at the bottom of the stairs. He'd made an important decision tonight and there would be no going back.

Chapter Five

STARING INTO THE mirror in one of the upstairs bathrooms, Amanda tried to repair her hair and makeup. The wind had teased her carefully pinned chignon apart and the brief spate of tears had smeared her mascara. She dabbed at her eyes with a tissue, her hands still trembling from her conversation with Seb. It wasn't fair how he kept bringing up the past and using it as a club to batter her heart.

She needed to get the hell out of here.

Stuffing the tissue back into her small purse, she gave her appearance one last perusal. Thankfully she looked almost normal. Only the most eagle-eyed observer would be able to see the traces of tears she'd artfully concealed.

She slid the chain strap of her purse onto her shoulder and twisted the doorknob, determined to find Darby so they could leave. Only when she was home and away from everyone would she feel safe again.

She jumped back when a large figure stood on the other side of the door. "Excuse me. I'm sorry."

Two masculine hands gripped her shoulders to steady her on the four inch heels she wore.

"Easy there. Are you okay?"

Dear God, she couldn't catch a break. Seb was standing right in front of her with a concerned expression, his fingers sending heat to every part of her body.

"I'm fine. I just didn't realize anyone was on the other side of the door, that's all." She took another step back to dislodge his hold but it only made things worse. One hand slid down her back while the other traveled up to her jaw, tracing it with his rough fingers.

"I came to talk to you."

The overwhelming pleasure of his touch was almost more than she could bear. She knew he could see the heightened color in her cheeks but could he hear the galloping of her heart? It sounded like a timpani in her ears, drowning out any of the noise from the party below.

"I'm okay." His massive frame was blocking her path. "If you will excuse me, Seb."

Instead of moving he stepped forward, forcing

her back into the bathroom. Swinging the door shut, he reached back and clicked the lock. She was now trapped in a small room with the man she'd loved more than anything or anyone in the world. If it weren't so tragic she might well be laughing.

Except that it was happening to her.

"We need to talk, Amanda. Honestly. The tension is so thick between us we could cut it with a knife. We're going to see each other from time to time. We have to be able to deal with it."

His declaration only served to turn her anguish to anger. Always the alpha male, he'd decided something so everyone had to fucking fall in line. She wasn't that naive little girl anymore who worshipped the ground he walked on. As a woman she could see his flaws along with all the wonderful qualities she'd fallen in love with.

"Did you follow me up here? I won't be bullied, Seb." Her fingers tightened on her purse to keep from smacking his too handsome face. He thought he had all the answers. This was the big reason they'd called off the wedding all those years ago. "Now let me out."

"No." His expression was implacable and he was rooted to the spot in front of the door. "Stop being so stubborn. We need to talk about us."

"There is no us," she hissed. "There hasn't been an *us* for many years. Did you get a head injury in Afghanistan and forget that we called off the wedding?"

Shit, now he'd done it. He had her babbling about things she'd never wanted to talk about again.

"It was my leg that was injured. My head is fine. My heart, on the other hand, isn't. There's still something between us, Mandy. I feel it and I know you do too. We can't ignore this."

Red hot anger rose up inside of her. Who in the fuck did he think he was? She wouldn't allow him to rock her carefully arranged world. She'd worked too hard to get to this place in her life.

"Really? I can. Watch me." She pushed at his body but wasn't able to budge him an inch. "Get the hell out of my way, Seb. I don't give a shit what you think is still between us. I'm done."

"I'm not moving, Mandy. I know you're mad at me. I know I was an arrogant asshole, among other things. I wasn't the man you needed me to be but I want to make up for that."

"Fuck you."

Amanda tried to squeeze past him but he simply lifted her up in his arms and deposited her on the vanity. She pummeled him with her fists and cracked his shin a few times with her high heel but he easily overcame her struggles, his strength far superior to her own.

"Calm down, Mandy." His cool voice only pissed her off even more. Gently he captured her wrists in one hand while his legs trapped her own against the cabinet. Reaching down, he slid her shoes from her feet. They fell to the floor with a thud that matched the pounding of her heart. Her breath was coming in shallow gasps and a flame was beginning to lick along her veins.

Seb knew what being helpless did to her. In their youth they'd experimented with sex and they'd found she had a predilection to be submissive. It was as if giving up control to him gave her permission to enjoy making love. A therapist she'd been seeing after her divorce had helped her make sense of it, but dammit—he was using it against her.

"Leave me the hell alone." She tried to wriggle free but he held her effortlessly. A smile was spreading across his face and she knew with certainty he was aware of her own arousal.

"I don't think that's what you want. I think you want something else."

Just because her body was begging for his didn't mean she had to listen. She'd pushed away her own physical needs for the better part of a decade before he'd waltzed back into her life. But he didn't give her a chance to protest, his lips crashing down on hers.

Claiming, dominating, his mouth gentled when she stopped struggling. His tongue rubbed and explored even as he held her immobile. Fire swept through her as honey drenched her panties. She didn't remember the last time she'd been this aroused, this needy. Her sex life with Emmett had been perfunctory at best but with Seb it had been… amazing.

She'd been alone too long, craving the long forgotten feeling of being desired.

With one kiss everything changed.

Chapter Six

W HEN SEB DRAGGED his lips from Amanda's the world he'd so carefully cultivated was blown to smithereens. His love for this woman had never died, no matter what he'd told himself all these years. This was the mate that had been created just for him and he wouldn't – couldn't – allow her to push him away.

But it wasn't going to be easy. He'd need to romance and woo her all over again, showing her she could trust him. He wasn't the same young man who had clumsily tried to dominate her life as a way of being grown up.

Hopefully he wasn't that naïve anymore.

Instead of being daunted by the uphill battle Seb faced, he was energized by it. Showing Amanda that he loved and respected her was a gift to be treasured, not a curse. All he needed was the second chance he'd never thought he'd get – or deserved.

He stared into her eyes, stormy with conflicted emotions. Already he could feel a wall building between them despite the soul-searing kiss of moments ago. He thought he'd destroyed it but in mere moments she'd built up a fortress stronger than ever.

She'd tried unsuccessfully to straighten her hair and had apparently given up, letting it hang in loose waves around her shoulders. At some point he'd run his fingers through those silky golden tresses. Her lips were swollen and her face glowed. Darby or any of the party-goers downstairs would take one look at her and know that she'd been kissed and kissed well.

"Let me drive you home," he offered, wanting to save her from that fate. If he'd been thinking straight this wouldn't have happened. Now that it had he couldn't regret it, but that didn't mean he'd lost all sensitivity for her feelings. He'd let his emotions override his good sense but he vowed right then not to let it happen again. Next time they kissed it would be Amanda's idea.

Seb pulled her into his arms and for a long moment she sagged against him, her face pressed against his chest. But the closeness and serenity didn't last long. She shook her head and stepped back, her arms crossed protectively over her chest.

"I can't do this again."

"Do what again?"

"This. All of this. I'm finally content with my life. I won't jeopardize everything I've worked so hard for. Not even for you." She swiped at her hair and tucked her purse under her arm, her hands trembling with emotion she obviously didn't want to admit.

"I don't want to take anything from you. I want us to build something new. Tell me everything you're afraid of," he offered. "Tell me and let's try to put the past behind us and create a new future. Tell me what you need me to do, Mandy."

"There's nothing you can do." Her voice had risen in the small space. "It's too late. Now please step aside. I have to get out of here."

He had no choice this time, not wanting to upset her further. As she passed him, he stopped her with a hand on her shoulder but she didn't look up and meet his gaze.

"Please let me drive you home. You're upset. You can slip out the back door and I'll meet you in the driveway."

"I'm going to find Darby and then I'm going home. Not with you. Leave me alone, Seb. There's nothing here for you. I'm not the person I used to be. Too much has happened."

After the kiss between them he didn't believe her, but she obviously needed some space to process everything. He opened the door and she brushed past him and out into the hall. Following at a discreet distance, he was surprised to see Darby climbing the stairs to intercept her.

The man took one look at Amanda and one look at Seb, who wasn't far behind. Clearly Darby knew what had been going on and he didn't look very happy about it. His arm went around Amanda's shoulders and he led her down the stairs, but not before throwing a warning look over his shoulder at Seb.

Warn away, buddy. Amanda had told him it was too late but she hadn't told him she didn't care. She might have changed but then so had he. He would do anything to win her love, and the battle began right here, right now.

AMANDA STAYED SILENT as Darby drove her home. He had, of course, figured out what had happened between her and Seb upstairs at the party. It was only then that she had realized why Seb had wanted to drive her home – "hot, passionate kiss" had been emblazoned across her forehead in big neon-colored letters. She'd kept her head down until they were out of the house but she was sure she'd received some strange looks on the way.

"I don't want you to see Sebastian again," Darby said abruptly, breaking the silence.

Appalled at the way he was speaking to her, she twisted in the seat so her back was to the door. "I don't think I appreciate your tone. I'm a grown woman and I make my own decisions."

After her fiasco of a marriage to Emmett no one was going to run her life ever again. Not even Sebastian Gibbs. If he thought he could swoop in and start bossing her around he had another think coming. And Darby? Since when did he bark out orders?

"You can't think clearly when it comes to that man. I thought you two would dance and you would tell him to go to hell. But things have taken a turn. You obviously need someone to talk some sense into you. I remember how things were when you two called off the wedding."

So did she. She'd gone on a spree of epic bad decision-making that had culminated in her divorce. The one good decision she'd made in the last thirteen years.

"I'm fine. Seb said one true thing tonight and that's that he and I need to make some sort of peace with each other. We've left this hanging between us too long."

Amanda didn't feel the need to justify her actions to Darby or anyone else. She was past that point in her life.

"You need to stay far away from him." The car swept into her driveway, the headlights illuminating the manicured lawn of her Mediterranean style home in a quiet suburb north of Clearwater. Darby put the car in park and killed the engine. "You kissed him tonight, didn't you?"

Unclipping the seatbelt, she pushed open the passenger door. "This conversation is over. Call me sometime if you can speak to me like an adult. I don't question your decisions and I expect the same courtesy."

Darby grabbed her arm and she jerked away. "I'm tired of being manhandled. Everyone thinks they can tell me what to do and I'm sick of it."

"Listen, I'm sorry." There was desperation and regret in Darby's tone. "I just don't want to see you go through it all again. Sebastian is bad news."

"I think you're being a little dramatic. Seb isn't evil."

"Is there any reason to see him again? You've avoided him all this time, after all."

"He's doing some pro bono legal work for the

foundation."

Amanda didn't mention that Seb had indicated he wanted to see her again, that he wanted to somehow make up for everything that had happened between them.

"Let your administrator handle this, Amanda." His voice gentled and his fingers brushed her own. "I'm your friend and I just want whatever is best for you, that's all."

"I know you do, and thank you for that. Good night." She swung her legs out of the car and he moved to open his door.

"Wait a minute and I'll walk you to the door."

She wanted to be alone to deal with all the colliding emotions inside.

"No, it's not even ten feet."

Not waiting for his reply, she quickly exited the car and jogged up the path to her front door. After she unlocked it she turned to wave to Darby who was still in his car. He looked put out but started the engine and reversed down the driveway. She'd deal with Darby and his hurt feelings another day. Probably by tomorrow he'd be onto something else, forgetting all about their conversation tonight.

Walking through the living room and kitchen she flipped on a few lights. Physically she was exhausted, but mentally her mind was way too active to be able to sleep anytime soon. She stopped at the refrigerator in her large, homey kitchen and grabbed a bottle of water and a few of the homemade cookies she'd made earlier that day from the plate on the counter before heading back into the master bedroom.

Placing the water bottle on the nightstand and holding a cookie in her mouth she stripped off her evening dress and panties, tossing them aside. They seemed to reek of kisses, Seb, and illicit passion. It was a concoction she hadn't experienced in a long time, although it was probably only her imagination.

Padding naked into the bathroom, she started a bath and poured in a few drops of oil before climbing in herself. She relaxed in the steamy water as it lapped at her chin and tried to make sense of what she'd done at the party and her swirling emotions.

The one thing Amanda had learned in therapy was to own her actions and decisions. She had allowed her need and passion for Seb to override her good judgment. It hadn't been smart but there was no going back.

Seb had said he wanted to talk about things, make some sense of the past. Her first reaction had been complete rejection of the offer but perhaps she'd been too hasty. It might be a good idea for them to finally talk as adults. Maybe this was the closure she needed to allow herself to move on. She'd spent so much time trying not to think about the past that the fact was she hadn't dealt with it all that well.

If Seb initiated more contact she would talk to him. Maybe she could finally put him – and her feelings – in the rearview mirror.

Chapter Seven

"**D**O YOU HAVE the Blum file?" Dane breezed into Seb's office with his usual smile. It was a Saturday morning and the office was quiet. Chris was at his parents' house in St. Augustine for the weekend so it was just Dane and Seb.

Seb dug his hand into a scattered stack and pulled out the file. "Right here."

Dane grimaced at the disorder of Seb's office. "How can you find anything in here? It looks like a grenade went off."

"I know where everything is. My organizational skills are deceptive but effective."

"Your organizational skills are non-existent," Dane retorted. "You forget I shared an apartment with you."

Seb, Dane, and Christian had been roommates all through Harvard undergrad and then Harvard Law. That was one of the reasons they knew each other so well. Seb could deal with clutter around him but Dane, on the other hand, was meticulous in everything whether it was his home or his grooming. Chris fell somewhere in the middle, as usual. He was the go-between whenever Seb got too casual or lackadaisical or Dane got too obsessive-compulsive.

"I could never forget that. You were a pain in the ass to live with."

"You're no fucking day at the beach yourself." Dane plopped down into a guest chair and stretched out his long legs. "Why are you here, anyway? We haven't been open for business long enough to be behind."

Seb shrugged and reached for his coffee cup. "I wanted to get a few things cleared away for Monday, that's all. I probably won't be here very long. What's your story?"

Dane held up the Blum file. "I got a call and they're ready to settle." He dug into the front pocket of his jeans. "That reminds me. You had a call this morning from a Lance Poplin—says he's ready to make a better offer. Whatever that means."

Dane tossed the paper on the desk and Seb picked it up, perusing it for any clues as to what the offer might be. Unfortunately the message was just as his friend had said and nothing more. Seb would have to call Poplin to find the details and then talk to Amanda. At least now he had a concrete reason to see her again.

"This is the developer that's trying to run Amanda and the women's shelter out of the house they purchased. Poplin wants the entire block for condos."

Dane snorted in derision. "Just what Florida needs—more condos. Shit, is real estate coming back again? All we need is another bubble to burst."

"It is," Seb said dryly, frowning at his now empty coffee cup. "He low-balled the first offer so I hope this one isn't a waste of my time."

"Is Amanda looking to sell?"

"She'd entertain the right offer." Seb got up and crossed the room to the coffee pot in the corner and poured himself another cup. He pointed to the spare mug on the counter but Dane shook his head. He was probably on one of his health kicks again.

"What about you? Is spending time with Amanda a good idea? Chris or I can take this over for you."

If it was possible Dane was even more protective than Chris, and declaring his intentions was going to upset his friend.

"Actually, we may have had a breakthrough last night. I think she still has feelings for me. And hell, you know how I feel about her—always have. I decided last night that I'm going for it. For her. I never thought I'd get a second chance but I really think this might be it. I won't pass it up."

"A breakthrough?" Dane sat up straight in the chair. "I don't even want to fucking know what kind of breakthrough you had, although by the smug-ass smile you have on your face this morning I can guess. But have you lost your mind, dude? What will you do if she tells you to take a hike? You're too old to go back into the Army and get yourself blown up or shot at because your heart is broken. Fuck, Seb—think this through."

Seb rubbed his thigh where that bullet had left a nasty scar, thinking of how he'd stayed up half the night thinking about this very thing. He was done thinking and it was time to take action.

"Trust me, I have. If Amanda blows me off, well, then I know for sure that it's not meant to be. But dammit, Dane, how can I walk away from this chance to be with the only woman I've ever loved? Could you do that?"

Dane stood and moved toward the door. "I've never been in love so I have no idea. Watching you, by the way, sure doesn't make me anxious to do it, either. It looks messy and painful so I'll just say no thanks. There are no shortage of willing women in this world. Shit, you don't need to marry them, Seb. Just throw them a diamond bracelet or some earrings every now and then. That keeps them happy and you out of divorce court. Repeat after me...community property."

Seb shook his head at his best friend. "When did you get so damn cynical?"

Dane just laughed and took the coffee cup out of Seb's hand. "Have you met my parents? I learned at the feet of experts. Put that swill away and let's go get some breakfast. Pancakes are on me."

Seb eyed Dane suspiciously. "Is this just a ruse to get me somewhere so you can talk me out of this? I won't change my mind."

"No way." Dane raised his hands in surrender. "I'm your friend, and if this is what you want then that's what I want. Hell, maybe I'll give you some pointers with the ladies that I've picked up over the years."

"Now this I've got to hear. Not that I plan to use any of them. It's purely for entertainment value."

"Listen and learn, bro. I'll get my keys and

we'll get out of here."

Dane loped down the hall whistling a song from their days in high school while Seb tried to straighten his desk for Monday morning. Despite the ribbing he'd given Dane, it might not be a bad idea to brainstorm some ideas to woo Amanda. It had been over a decade since Seb had given a damn whether a woman cared or not. This was too important to mess up.

IT WAS SIMPLY another quiet Sunday night for Amanda. She knew most of her friends would have called it boring, but she enjoyed puttering around the house in old clothes and no makeup. She'd worked in the back yard this morning and then lazed in the pool in the afternoon. Now she was showered, her stomach was growling, and the contents of her refrigerator left something to be desired. She'd already eaten her weight in chocolate chip cookies. She needed real food. Delivery might be her only option for sustenance. She was sifting through pizza coupons when she heard pounding on her front door.

"Just a minute," she called out, making a face at her cut-off shorts and tank top. No bra. Crap. She hated the damn things and never wore one when she was home. She'd just have to cover up. Picking up the stack of coupons, she held them against her chest and went to answer the door.

Peeking out the window, her heart lurched in her chest.

Seb.

Or more correctly, Seb with a couple of large brown paper bags and a bouquet of flowers in his arms.

He hadn't given her much time to rebuild her defenses and she was sure that was by design. She'd hoped to be more put together when they had their talk. It looked like that wasn't going to be an option; for as much as she didn't want to answer the door, a big part of her did—that hopeful, optimistic person deep inside of her that wanted to believe everything was rainbows and unicorns.

That person kept getting Amanda in deep shit.

Steeling herself for what was ahead, she opened the door and stepped back. "Hello, Seb. This is a surprise."

The wonderful smell of garlic and tomato sauce wafted from the bags and her stomach gurgled loudly, making Seb laugh and her to press her hand to her stomach. That only served to uncover her already hard nipples under the cotton of her tank.

Fuckity fuck.

"I brought dinner. I was going to say that I hope you're hungry, but that appears to be a given."

His golden brown eyes had darkened as his gaze swept up and down her body before coming to rest on her breasts that seemed to swell under his regard.

"You should have called."

Amanda was going to let him in but some impish demon inside wanted to give him some shit first. As always, Seb made the decisions and she was supposed to just fall in line. He needed to learn she wasn't planning to do that again. Ever.

"I should have and I apologize." He nodded in an almost humble manner which was completely incongruent with everything she knew about this man. In all their time together he'd never apologized for anything or even admitted when he was wrong. "Lance Poplin called with another offer and I thought we could discuss it over dinner."

"And?" she prompted. "Is that all you want to talk about?"

He heaved a big sigh but a smile played on that gorgeous mouth of his. "Okay, maybe I wanted to talk about us a little bit. Are you going to let me in?"

She took a few more steps back so he could cross the threshold. "Only because you have food and I'm starving. I was about to order a pizza."

Seb laughed and headed straight for her kitchen. "That answers my first question. Your eating habits are as appalling as they were thirteen years ago. Just in case, I brought a wide selection."

"I resent that remark. My diet is much better than it was."

Amanda rummaged through the cabinets for plates, silverware, and napkins while he unpacked the food, then she filled a vase with water for the flowers. She leaned in and breathed in their scent, eyeing him warily over the fragrant buds. She shouldn't let a bouquet of simple posies soften her up, but it did feel nice that he'd gone to the trouble.

"Really? When was the last time you ate a vegetable?" Steam rose from the food as Seb lifted the lids. "Too slow. If you have to think about it it's been too long."

Some things never changed. Seb had always given her crap about her eating habits, not that he was a whole lot better. The only difference was he was willing to eat green things and she wasn't.

"I had corn on Wednesday," she said with as much dignity as she could muster. Their bantering brought back many happy memories and for once she didn't shove them away. If this was closure on the past, she might as well embrace all of it – good and bad.

Seb snorted and they sat down at the table opposite one another. "Corn is not a vegetable and neither are potatoes. They're a starch. I'm talking green, Mandy. When was the last time you ate a green vegetable?"

"I think I was about five," she conceded. "Now what did you bring? Is that lasagna?"

"It is." Seb pointed to another container. "Chicken parmesan, and this one over here is fettuccine alfredo. There's also salad and garlic bread." He sighed in resignation. "You don't eat salad, do you?"

"Pasta salad," she said, hopping up from the table. "Wait, I forgot drinks. What would you like? I have water, ginger ale, milk, orange juice, or iced tea."

"Ginger ale."

She grabbed two cans from the refrigerator and re-joined him at the table. They ate in silence for a few minutes, but once her stomach began to feel satisfied the rest of her wasn't.

"You wanted to talk about an offer," she prompted.

Seb placed his fork on the edge of his plate.

"For starters. I talked to Poplin yesterday and the new offer is significantly better at twenty percent over market. Plus he's willing to pay any relocation fees. Is that good enough to think about?"

"It is. I'm just surprised he made another attempt. Can I have some time to discuss it with the staff?"

"Absolutely. He won't wait forever but he'll wait a few days." Seb sat back in the chair. "Now let's talk about us."

"Us?" she echoed, her stomach fluttering with nervousness. Actually discussing this with him was more than scary. It was terrifying.

"Yes, us. And more specifically what future we may have."

"What makes you think we have any sort of future?"

She needed to stop repeating things like an idiot but she couldn't help herself. She hadn't been prepared for this. They didn't have a future. Did they? She'd planned on bringing closure to their relationship, not continuing on.

She was too afraid to let herself feel hope for the first time in a very long while. There were so many obstacles between them. So many things he didn't know. She couldn't allow herself to trust him. Not yet. Maybe not ever.

Chapter Eight

"I THINK THAT we can have one if we try and put the past behind us." Seb felt the weight of the world on his shoulders. His future happiness might hinge on this exact moment. "A fresh start for both of us. A new relationship with a new dynamic. Two different people who still have feelings for one another. And don't tell me that you don't, Mandy. I wouldn't believe it."

Amanda fiddled with her fork, the pattern on the flatware elegantly simple. Quite different than what both of them had been brought up in. In fact, her entire home was almost an anti-stance against her childhood. He'd taken in the comfortably elegant decor the minute she'd let him past the threshold. Did she know it spoke volumes about the person she was without her saying a word?

The kitchen was oversized with country white

cabinets and a large granite island in the middle. The living room had beige leather furniture and light oak tables with wide-plank honey maple floors. No Swarovski chandeliers, no Chippendale originals, no furniture that was purchased more for its value than for its comfort and utility.

This home stated loudly and clearly that Amanda didn't live to socialize or gather material possessions.

"We don't even really know each other anymore. You think you know me but you don't. Not really."

They were different people but deep down they hadn't changed. Their morals, values, and goals were still the same.

"Then let's get to know one another again. Give me a chance to show you that things can be better this time. That I'm a better man that's more worthy of you. Seb 2.0, if you will."

He'd tried to make a joke but Amanda only smiled slightly. "Before I can even think about going forward I think we need to clear the air about the past. It was a mutual decision to call off the wedding, Seb, but we never really talked about it afterward. You just…left."

"You want to talk about it now? I'm willing to do that. Are you?"

Her features were composed but her hands were shaking slightly as she set down her fork and met his gaze head on. "I know why I called off the wedding but what's your story? Why did you really call it off? Was there someone else? Did you fall out of love with me?"

Seb took a drink of his ginger ale before he tried to answer. The moment was here.

"There was no one else, I swear." He didn't imagine that her shoulders relaxed. "I didn't fall out of love with you. The fact is I've always loved you. I've never stopped."

Amanda hopped up from her chair, her blue eyes almost gray. "That's bullshit. If it were true you wouldn't have called off the wedding. If you're not going to tell me the truth you can leave."

Seb stood and grabbed her shoulders to turn her toward him. Their gazes clashed, her lips trembling. He had to find the right words. "I called off the wedding because I wasn't ready for the responsibility of marriage, Mandy. I was afraid. And if you are honest, you weren't ready either."

Her brow knitted as she processed his words. "We could have postponed the wedding, Seb. We could have waited a few more years if you felt that way."

Seb shook his head with a grim smile. "Are you

sure? What would your reaction have been if I'd said I needed a few more years?" His hands fell away and he took a deep breath. "Actually I know what your reaction was. You were angry and frustrated with me all the time and I didn't know how to fix that. So I left."

Amanda rubbed at her temples, conflict clearly showing in her features. "Even after we agreed to call it off I thought you'd be in my life. I never thought you'd just disappear. I guess I thought you'd come back and we'd both apologize and we'd work it all out."

"How can I explain what was going on in my head?" He scraped a hand through his hair in frustration. "I was trying to be the man in the relationship, or what I thought the man was supposed to be. Now I see that I wasn't being so much a man but a jerk. I tried to push you into doing everything my way and of course you rebelled. That just frustrated me all the more. Dammit, Mandy, you were so young."

Amanda grabbed her soda and took a drink, her lips pressed together. "What does my youth have to do with this? I was twenty. Hardly a child, Seb."

"Hardly a woman, either," he replied, needing to put his emotions into words. It wasn't easy.

He'd been ignoring his feelings for too many years. "I was already twenty-five, and you looked up to me to care for you. Fuck, who am I kidding? I loved the fact that you admired me, that you leaned on me. It made me feel special. It made me feel like a man. But it also scared the hell out of me. I thought it made sense at the time but it sounds stupid now."

"Yes, it does." Amanda's voice was tight with emotion. Whether it was anger or regret, Seb couldn't be sure.

"Dane, Chris, and I had just finished law school and were studying for the bar. Then 9/11. Hell, I don't know how to explain this. You always seemed so innocent and naive. I didn't want anything bad to touch you. I wanted to protect you. But I didn't really have a clue what that meant. I just couldn't admit it at the time."

Slapping the can down on the table, she whirled toward him, her face red with anger. "Once again the great Sebastian Gibbs makes all the decisions. Pulls all the strings. Amanda's just along for the ride."

"Then why did you call off the wedding, Mandy? It wasn't my idea originally. You were the first one to bring it up."

Her eyes went wide with shock and she shook

her head. "That's not true. It can't be true."

"Not that it matters who brought it up first, but yes, it was you. You said you didn't want to go back to school and I said you should. Then you said you didn't want to be a wife that wasn't with her husband and if you couldn't follow me then maybe we shouldn't get married at all."

"It was me?" Her words came out in a whisper, tears shimmering in her eyes. "Oh God. I remember it now. Funny, all these years I've blamed you. I thought you didn't love me anymore."

Her last words came out more as a sob and she turned her back to him, her arms wrapped around her torso. He wanted to go to her, comfort her, but he hadn't yet earned that right.

"I've always loved you. But love wasn't enough for us back then. It wasn't our time."

She looked over her shoulder, her chin lifted in defiance even as her eyes were bright with tears. "And you think the time for us is now? I may still have feelings for you, Seb, but I won't go back to what we had before. I won't be bossed around by you anymore. I'm tired of the men in my life thinking they can make decisions for me."

"I'm sorry about how I treated you before. As I said, I want a new start for us and that includes a new dynamic. I was wrong and I've learned that I don't need to control you to be the man in the relationship. To care for you. I'm asking you to forgive me, Mandy."

He could hear his heart pounding in his ears and he shoved his hands in his pockets so she wouldn't see them shake. Everything was on the line here and one word from her could send him to heaven or hell.

It was her decision this time and for once he wouldn't push. He'd stated his case and now she was the judge and jury.

"I'm not sure I know this Seb before me. He's never apologized before."

"I'm sorry about that too. I was an arrogant SOB that needed to be taken down a peg or two, which the Army was happy to do. Will you accept my apology?"

He didn't realize he was holding his breath until she nodded. "I do. But I wish we could have worked this out back then. I loved you."

Her voice was urgent and something inside of Seb stirred at the sincerity in her tone. If she'd loved him that much then, would it be too much to ask for the chance to try and win it again?

"I'm not sure we were capable of working it out then. We were a couple of kids playing house, really. We didn't have a clue as to what we were doing or what those marriage vows truly meant." She started to protest but he held up his hand. He needed to get this out in the open. "Okay, maybe you did but I didn't. I didn't know what true commitment was. I knew I loved you and wanted you but let's face it, we'd never had any hard times to test that love, did we?"

To his shock Amanda began to laugh, a few tears leaking from her eyes. "No, we didn't. I've thought about that over the years. Our lives were too perfect, too easy. Until that day…"

Seb turned her so she was looking into his eyes. "I think deep inside we both knew we weren't ready and we took the easiest route out of the wedding…blaming each other. But it didn't take me very long to realize that my own shortcomings didn't have a thing to do with you and everything to do with me."

Amanda scrubbed at her tear-stained cheeks. "Somewhere in the back of my mind I thought you didn't want to marry me because I argued with you. I thought maybe you found someone that was happy to let you give the orders."

"You were never lacking in any way. I was an arrogant asshole," he stated, not even trying to sugarcoat the facts. "I'm still pretty arrogant but when it comes to you I'm a humbled man. Nothing I do can ever make that up, but I still love you, Mandy. I'm asking you for another chance. A new chance. I think deep down you still have feelings for me—at least you did when you kissed me at the party."

Red stained her cheeks and she quickly averted her eyes. "It was out of habit."

"Hell of a habit. Do you kiss everyone you dance with?"

Seb wasn't going to let her wriggle out of this. What they'd had two nights ago had been real.

"Of course not. I just…" Shaking her head, she plopped down into a chair. "Being back with you throws me off balance, that's all. I can't let you run my life, Seb. I've been down that road and I won't go there again."

"I'm not asking you to. I want us to be partners."

She finally looked up at him, and the fear in her expression made him want to reach out and pull her into his arms. He wanted to protect her from anything hurting her ever again. But he wouldn't make that mistake once more.

"So you don't care about being a dominant anymore?"

He'd wondered when she was going to get around to asking that.

"What I like in the bedroom is completely separate from the way I live my everyday life. You know I like being in charge in the bedroom. My problem was that I carried it into the rest of our relationship and acted like a dick. But if you ask me to choose between you and being dominant in the sack? I'd choose you every time. Hands down. No contest. It's just not that important to me. That's not what I need to feel like a grown man."

"What do you need to feel that way now?"

"To know that I've made the woman in my life happy and secure. That she knows that I love and adore her and will always put her first. That's what a man does."

Her lips trembled and she blinked away more tears, giving him hope that he'd somehow managed to touch her heart. She sat down heavily into a kitchen chair, pushing her hair away from her face.

"You're right. In my heart of hearts I know that calling off the wedding was the right thing to do. Neither of us was ready for it. I was living in a romantic fantasy world. The way I'd pictured our life is laughable now, like some 1950s sitcom. I had no sense of what adults do. Heck, I didn't even know how to balance my checkbook." She fiddled with the soda can on the table. "So now we're grown ups. So now we put the past behind us, bless it and release it. What happens then?"

Kneeling down in front of her chair he took her hands in his, feeling her pulse beat wildly under this thumb. His own heart was pounding hard and fast. "Start again. Replace the bad memories with good ones. I can't fix what's happened before but I can vow that I'll try to make the future the best it can be."

"I'm not sure I can believe in this. I mean it, Seb. I won't be treated like a child. If you do it again, that's it. I've come too far to go back."

Seb chuckled not at her words but at her tone. This woman meant business and he had to admit he admired the backbone she'd grown while they were apart. "I think you'd have my balls in a jar on the mantle if I tried it again."

Her lips quirked up into a smile and she looked so goddamn beautiful it almost took his breath away. He couldn't believe life had given him another chance to win this woman.

"You bet I would." She shook her head and leaned her forehead on her hand. "I didn't expect tonight to turn out this way. I thought we would talk, and I would probably cry. Then we would make some stupid pact about putting the past behind us and try to be friends or something.

Anything but this."

His hands cupped her face and his lips hovered above hers.

"The night is not over yet. In fact, it's just begun. Everything is new."

Chapter Nine

EVERYTHING WAS HAPPENING so fast. Amanda could barely catch her breath at the speed in which the evening had turned from closure to anything but. She had to be crazy to do this. Insane. But this was Seb, the man she'd loved since she was fourteen years old. Of course he hadn't known about her teenage crush, but when she'd turned eighteen and graduated high school he'd finally asked her out. It was with him on a hot summer night that she'd gladly surrendered her virginity. A night very much like tonight.

It had also been with him that she'd learned about all the different ways to have sex. They'd been like two kids in a candy store as they'd explored all the ways to bring pleasure to one another. But it had been the day he'd tied her up that had changed everything.

"I'm not ready to make love to you tonight,"

she whispered as his lips brushed her own, sending tingles straight to her southerly regions. "Not yet."

He didn't answer, instead deepening the kiss, his tongue exploring as if it was the first time they'd ever kissed. He was taking this new thing very seriously. When he finally lifted his head his brown eyes were soft with arousal.

"I'll wait as long as you need me to. Nothing is more important to me than us having a future together." His fingers brushed her cheek, leaving a trail of heat on her skin. "I plan to show you over the coming days and weeks. If you'll allow me to."

This was a whole new Sebastian. The man she'd known had been loving, kind, but more than sure of himself. Seeing him this way melted the ice around her heart too quickly and too soon. She wasn't quite ready to believe in this transformation no matter how much she wanted to.

"You want to date?" They'd dated and been engaged so it seemed strange to take a step back.

"Absolutely. I want us to get to know each other again." His hands slid up her arms to rest on her shoulders. "Let's have fun together. I know I could use it and I bet you could too."

Amanda couldn't argue with his logic. Fun had been in short supply these last few years and she wasn't normally a serious, melancholy person. At one point in the past people had described her as having a zest for life. But that young woman was long gone, beaten down by heartache and disappointment.

"Dating and fun? I guess that doesn't sound to onerous." Amanda found herself smiling as pleasant memories of the past flitted through her mind. "When do we start?"

Seb grinned and pulled her into a hug, his warm scent making the room spin and tilt. "We already have. We had dinner and now it's time for a movie. Your choice."

"I might pick some chick flick—are you sure you want me to choose?"

"Positive. I don't care what we see as long as I get to spend time with you."

Amanda was going to test that statement and Seb's intentions. She had to be sure he really meant it.

AMANDA'S BRIGHT RED golf ball slid between the rotating blades of the windmill but ran out of steam shortly after, leaving at least three feet to the hole. Seb might want to win her love again but he clearly wasn't going to go easy on her in a miniature golf game.

He was beating the pants off of her.

Not literally of course, but then after the last several dates they'd had it wasn't completely out of the question. They'd swam, seen movies, had a picnic, gone horseback riding, and tonight they were playing mini-golf at a jungle themed course in Clearwater. Seb had promised fun and delivered in spades.

After each date her resolve to keep him at arm's length would weaken a little more until now it lay in tatters, ripped and destroyed. So far Seb was keeping his promise not to run over her opinions with his own. It was a partnership she hadn't believed possible.

"Good shot." Seb dropped a kiss on her nose before lining up his own, the ball mere inches from the hole.

"It was a lousy shot. I suck. How did I let you talk me into this?" Amanda teased as he sunk the putt easily.

"Susie told me you liked playing miniature golf."

Susie was Amanda's best friend and business partner who was also most definitely on Seb's side. She'd been feeding him information about Amanda's likes and dislikes all week, making it very difficult to resist him.

"I do. When I'm playing against Susie. She sucks worse than I do."

Seb laughed and wrote down his score on a card with one of those tiny pencils. "So you only want to play games you'll win. Good to know. Is there anything else I should strike off my list?"

Amanda lined up the putt and struck the ball. Too hard. It careened off the wooden edge and landed on the other side of the hole about four feet away.

Well, shit.

"Monopoly. Gin Rummy. Poker. Blackjack. Basically all card and board games really. I'm much better at losing in sports, though. If you beat me in a foot race I could care less."

"The only place I'd be chasing you is in the bedroom—around the bed, that is."

The words were tinged with amusement and her cheeks burned with embarrassment as an image of Seb capturing her after a merry chase through the house danced through her imagination. Maybe even giving her a good, hard spanking. It had been too long since she'd had one of those.

"We shouldn't talk about that."

Mostly because she couldn't stop thinking about it as it was. Add in talking and she was near obsessive levels. Since the day she'd seen Seb that first time in his office she'd been tormented with visions of the two of them together doing what they'd done so very well thirteen years ago. There was no doubt it would be more than good.

That made Seb laugh all the harder. He leaned down close to her ear so no one else could listen in. "You can tell me we can't make love, but you can't tell me not to think about it. I think about it all the time when we're together."

"I just want to make sure that we don't make the same mistakes again. I don't want to end up where we were before."

His expression sobered and he ran his finger along her cheek, leaving a trail of heat in his wake. "I don't want that either. I'm in this for the long haul, Mandy. I want that lifetime together that we talked about so much."

A lifetime was something she wanted to believe in. "Then talk to me. Really talk to me. Tell me what changed you."

A strange expression passed across his face but was quickly gone. "A man has nothing but time to think when he's lying in an Army hospital. I thought about every day we'd spent together. Every conversation. Every single one. And I didn't like what I saw. I'd been arrogant and pushy, trying to run your life when I wasn't qualified to run my own. My only excuse is that I loved you so much and wanted to take care of you."

"Now you know I can take care of myself," Amanda said softly. She had regrets as well. As a young woman – girl, really – she hadn't handled things very maturely, always nagging and complaining instead of talking. It was amazing they'd stayed together as long as they had.

"You sure can." Seb grinned and swung the putter over his shoulder. "That's why I'm going to have no guilt whatsoever about playing to win."

"Give it your best shot. I'd rather lose honestly than win because you didn't try."

Honesty was the name of the game from now on. But she still had a few secrets he didn't know about.

She had to tell him. Soon.

Chapter Ten

SEB PICKED UP the heavy photo album from Amanda's coffee table, smiling as he paged through it. Pictures of Amanda as a golden-haired cherub dressed in pink, then later as a radiant teenager on Seb's arm before they left for the senior prom. She'd worn a black taffeta dress that had shown off a few inches of cleavage which had scandalized her mother, but Seb had really appreciated. Both he and Amanda were wearing bright smiles that appeared amazingly naïve all these years later.

Those two kids hadn't known a fucking thing about life.

"Don't we look so young?" Amanda sat down next to Seb, holding two wine glasses, one of which she handed to him. "I pulled that out last night. I hadn't looked at it in years."

Probably for good reason. Living too much in

the past wasn't a good thing but these pictures held wonderful memories of those innocent early years.

"We look like we didn't have a care in the world, which we didn't," Seb observed. "You were right. Our lives were way too easy back then. We didn't have a clue what we were in for."

"I was completely unprepared for the reality of being a grown up. It was too much like a fairy tale except for that happily ever after stuff. I think we all learned the truth about that."

She'd been through so much after they'd broken up but she didn't act bitter. Her attitude was one of calm acceptance and cool control. He didn't know the whole story about the last thirteen years but he did know that this Amanda wasn't the type who was going to let him dictate anything to her – from how she lived her life right down to what movie they were going to see.

She'd grown into a strong, independent woman.

And he'd finally grown into a man that thought it was sexy as hell.

He turned the page and his heart jumped and his breath caught in his throat. It was a picture of the day he'd proposed. She was holding up her hand with the diamond ring on it and they were both laughing and smiling.

"I remember that day," Amanda said softly, her fingers tightening on his thigh. "We were so happy. Everyone was – our friends, our family. I thought everything would be perfect from that moment on."

Her cheeks were pink and her gaze was focused on her toes. His own heart squeezed in his chest as his own inadequacy came rushing back. "I wish with all my heart I could have made life perfect for you, Mandy. I felt like such a failure when I left."

Her head shot up, a frown on her beautiful face. "Nothing is perfect, Seb. Nothing. I know you tried to do that. And I know that I made your life difficult by not understanding that it was me pushing you to do it in the first place. I wanted you to be some knight in shining armor saving me from having to actually make hard decisions and struggle." She cupped his cheek, caressing his jaw, her fingers warm wherever they touched. "I forced you to act more like a father or big brother and then resented it when you did. You apologized to me but I've never apologized to you. I'm sorry I did that, Seb. It was wrong but I was young and dumb and didn't realize what I was doing. But I do now."

Unshed tears brightened her eyes and her lips

trembled with an emotion he knew all too well. Regret. They needed to put a stake in its heart and bury it. Nothing productive came from it.

"Thank you for apologizing but you didn't have to. We both did some stupid things but I think we've grown and changed. I know I have, and that's what I hope to prove to you."

Her fingers trailed down his neck to his chest, her palm covering his galloping heart. "You have. I'd forgotten what it was like to be this happy and with someone I trust as much as you."

The room spun for a moment before righting itself. "Then you believe me when I say that I love you?"

Amanda nodded and then smiled playfully. "I could use a little more persuading. Maybe a more...hands-on approach?"

A grin spread across Seb's face. He knew this mood well and it always meant fun. And pleasure.

"I think I can manage that. But I need to know something first. I know you want us to be partners in life but what about the bedroom? How do you feel about that?"

She fiddled with the hem of her shorts. "I haven't done anything like that since we were together."

He didn't allow disappointment to take hold,

pushing it ruthlessly away. Just being with Amanda was enough. He didn't have to play the Dom too.

"Then we'll go vanilla," he stated, scooping her into his arms and onto his lap. "It will still be amazing."

"No, wait." Amanda shook her head, her cheeks having gone from pink to bright red. "I...I want it all."

Blood rushed through Seb's veins straight to his cock, which was pushing against his fly. "All? Are you sure? We don't have to do any of that, sweetheart."

She didn't want to talk about her sex life after him but it needed to be done. "I am sure. Have you...?"

Amanda didn't want to hear about the women he'd been with but the question had slipped out before she'd been able to stop it. If they were going to have a conversation about their sex partners she wasn't sure how she'd handle it. Her sex life with Emmett had been, in a word, terrible.

"Not with all women." Seb shook his head and placed a soft kiss at the corner of her mouth. "I have visited some clubs and learned a few things about being a Dominant. I hope to God I'm better at it now."

He hesitated, obviously not sure whether he

should say something. "And?" she prompted him.

"Was your ex-husband your Dom?" he asked, his lips twisting as if he'd said something really unpleasant. The thought of Emmett being a Dom or even giving a shit about her pleasure was completely laughable.

"No," she said firmly. She wouldn't go into the details but she could reveal this much. "Honestly, Emmett and I didn't have a very good sex life. We weren't...compatible in that way."

"I don't know whether to be happy or sad. I guess if I were any kind of man I'd be sorry that things weren't good for you. That you didn't get what you needed."

If it had crossed her mind to tell him the sordid details about her marriage, his last statement stopped the idea cold. There would be another day for the story. She didn't want to ruin their new beginning.

"Make me happy tonight." Amanda marveled at her boldness, but then this was Seb. He hadn't allowed her to be shy around him for very long.

His grin warmed her heart and made her tingle all over. "Do you remember how we start, Mandy?"

She nodded, her entire body starting to tremble with arousal. How many nights had she lain awake reliving making love with Seb? Too many to count. The dreams had been vivid, high-def images. She'd been able to hear their moans and whispers, smell the scent of sex, all of it designed to torture her and keep her from moving on.

On shaky knees she stood and walked back to the bedroom. She stripped her clothes off and then turned the bed down so the covers were folded at the end of the mattress. After lighting some candles she turned the lights off, enjoying the flickering shadows on the wall. A hint of vanilla began to permeate the air and she knelt down beside the bed on the area rug, exhaling slowly and trying to control her racing heart.

A cool breeze from the vent tightened her nipples even as heat was building inside. She waited in position, closing her eyes and listening to the thump of her heart and nothing else. A sense of calm spread through her as she visualized her and Seb together. Happy—the past no longer a factor. She wanted it. She didn't know if it was possible but she wasn't too proud to admit that she needed to be loved.

"Good girl." Seb was standing next to her, his hand on her head, his fingers stroking her hair. "Let's go over the rules, just in case. Rule one. I am in charge. The only decision you need to make is whether to use your safeword. I realize you didn't have one before, but I think it's a good idea to have one now."

Instantly alert, she lifted her head to look up at him. Was he planning to hurt her tonight? Seb shook his head, apparently reading her expression of alarm.

"Relax, sweetheart. I'm not a sadist. But we haven't been together like this in a long time. I think it's a good idea to have a stop mechanism in case I go somewhere you're not comfortable with."

She nodded in agreement. "You're right. Can I pick anything I want?"

"It's your safeword." Seb gave her a playful smile.

"Hmmm…how about 'champagne'?" Amanda giggled at the thought of yelling the word at the top of her lungs.

"Champagne it is," Seb agreed. "Now, rule number two. You do not come without my permission. And finally, rule number three. Do you remember that rule?"

She did remember it. It had been the hardest one to follow. "No feeling ashamed or guilty about what we do together and enjoy."

"That's right. Now let's get started. Open my pants and take out my cock."

She loved it when he had that deep, commanding tone to his voice. Her body responded instantly to it, a deep flush covering her bare skin and a bar of arousal building in her abdomen. She reached up and slid the button free and pulled the tab of the zipper down exposing his ridged stomach, a silky trail of blond hair disappearing under the waistband of his boxers. Sliding the elastic out of the way, her fingers wrapped around his thick cock, pulling it free from the fabric. Her first instinct was to lick the mushroom head and trace the blue and purple veins with her tongue, but then she remembered that she wasn't in charge at the moment.

Seb was in control.

She had no decisions to make. Nothing to worry about. Her mind wouldn't be busy wondering whether he liked what she was doing because whatever she was doing would be what he'd ordered her to do. If he didn't like what she was doing he would simply command her to do something else. No muss, no fuss. All she had to do was obey and feel. It was such a luxury and one she had honestly missed.

Her hands brushed his bare thighs and her fingers felt the ridged outline of the scar where he'd been shot. In London, she hadn't known about it when it happened but had heard about it later. She'd had to quell the urge to run to him and nurse him better despite everything that had passed between them. His very real mortality had terrified her, bringing the danger he was in every day to the forefront of her mind. In truth, she hadn't breathed easily until he'd left the Army almost a year ago.

Now he was here in one piece, alive and well.

Peeking up at him from under her lashes, she sat back on her heels and waited for his direction. He didn't make her wait long. Sinking his fingers into her hair, he guided her head until her lips were directly in front of his cock.

"Suck me."

Not needing to be told twice, Amanda wet her lips hungrily before starting at the base and licking in long swipes all the way to the head. She fluttered her tongue around the slit, knowing how sensitive Seb was there and was rewarded with his fingers tightening in her hair and the sound of his breath coming out in a hiss. She might be the one on her knees but at this moment she felt very powerful indeed.

Opening her jaws wide she engulfed the head with her mouth, letting her tongue flicker even as she sealed her lips tightly and began to bob her head up and down.

"Son of a fucking bitch."

She would have smiled at his hoarse expletive but her mouth was already busy. She gave him no quarter, relentless with her lips and tongue until she felt him swell inside her mouth, the hand buried in her hair twisting painfully. His hot seed jetted to the back of her throat and she had to swallow quickly not to miss a drop. She used her tongue to clean him when he was done before sitting back on her heels, a feeling of triumph percolating inside.

It had been so long since she'd felt good with a man in a sexual situation. Amanda had almost come to expect the feeling of awkwardness and inadequacy that had dogged her relationships since Seb. But not today. Seb made her feel sexy and wanted.

"I'd forgotten how lethal that mouth of yours was," Seb chuckled, pulling his pants up but leaving them unzipped. He lifted her chin with his fingers so she could see the satisfied smile on his face. "I can't go all night like I could in my early twenties but I think I'm still good for another go this evening. Maybe more. I'm not that old."

His rough fingers caressed her cheek and she leaned her head against his palm. "Thank you,

Sir."

"You're welcome, sweetheart. Are you ready to have some fun?"

"Yes, Sir," she responded, wanting to show him her submission and that she accepted his leadership.

"Time for your spanking then."

His lips were curved into a grin and his brown eyes sparkled with mischief. Sparks lit inside at the thought of being draped over his knee, his large hand warming up her ass cheeks. Her nipples tightened and even more honey dripped from her pussy. But...what had she done to deserve punishment?

"I don't understand, Sir. What am I being punished for? What did I do?"

"Nothing. This wouldn't be a punishment."

Amanda frowned. "Then what would the spanking be for?"

"For fun," he said firmly. "For no other reason than I know you enjoy it."

She couldn't argue the fact nor did she want to.

What she wanted was a spanking. Seb was the only man in the world she would ever allow to do this.

"Yes, Sir." She kept her eyes down and placed

her hands behind her back as she had read in several smutty books on her e-reader. When she couldn't submit in reality she'd moved over to fantasy.

"What a good girl you are," Seb praised as he sat down on the bed and patted his lap. "Come here then and get what you need."

Rising swiftly she draped herself over his knees, her palms and toes on the floor and her bottom up in the air. Or at least it felt like it. His hands rubbed circles on the sensitive skin, warming up the flesh and making her quiver in anticipation.

"When was the last time you had a spanking, sweetheart?"

His fingers had slipped down into her slit and she moaned as he brushed her clit. It sent a rush of cream onto his hand and her thighs.

"Um, with you, Sir."

She hated admitting it but she couldn't lie to him about something like this. His hand paused as if he was surprised by her answer, but then he gave her bottom a light smack.

"Then you are far overdue. We'll start light and work our way up. No set count since this is just for our mutual pleasure. Don't hesitate to use your safeword, especially as it's been so long since your last discipline."

Her heart galloping in her chest and her breathing shallow, she waited for what seemed like an eternity for the first impact of his palm on her ass. When it finally came it was lighter than she expected, barely stinging the skin but still upping the temperature on her bottom. The blows continued growing progressively harder until she was wriggling on his knees. Her butt cheeks had to be glowing red and her hand flew behind her to ward him off, but he simply chuckled and anchored her wrist at the small of her back with his left hand.

"Do you need to use your safeword, Mandy?" Seb paused, waiting for her answer. The last thing she wanted was for him to stop. She'd needed this for so long and hadn't even realized it.

"No, Sir."

Her voice was rusty but she must have said the words clearly enough as he began peppering her ass with measured smacks designed to heat the skin and send her pleasure-pain receptors into overdrive. Her mind, always busy with all the things she needed to think about and do, became clear and uncluttered, allowing her to sink into the moment and just feel. Nothing else existed but the two of them.

She was so lost to him that it took her a minute to realize the spanking was over and he was trailing his fingers through her drenched pussy. Skillful fingers circled her clit and her whole body shook as she tried to hold back her orgasm.

"Come."

The command was simple and direct but her body didn't need any second bidding. She exploded from the inside out, the room spinning and the lights dancing. She was still in its throes when he laid her stomach down on the edge of the bed and thrust hard inside of her from behind.

The feeling of being impaled on his cock was too much and her climax started all over again even as he began to piston in and out, hard and fast. No mercy, no quarter. Not that she wanted any. Amanda reveled in the way he used her for his pleasure as it never ceased to give her pleasure as well.

Seb's cock slammed into her over and over, never letting her down from the pinnacle. When he reached around and gave her already swollen clit a pinch she screamed as another orgasm roared mercilessly through her. It left her weak and shaking even as she heard his own groan and felt the heat of his seed deep inside.

Amanda's eyes swam with tears and they rolled down her cheeks, washing away so much of the baggage she'd been carrying with her all these years. With a muttered oath Seb gathered her into his arms, rocking her until she was sniffling, her fingers swiping at the wet skin.

"Aw baby, tell me what's wrong. What can I fix for you? Was I too rough?" Her cheek was pressed against his chest and she could hear the words rumble under her ear.

"I'm not sad. I'm happy." She hiccupped and accepted a fresh tissue from Seb.

"If I live to be a hundred and one years old I don't think I'll ever understand women. Are you sure you're okay?" She could hear the exasperation in his voice tinged with amusement.

She dabbed at her eyes and looked up at him, giving him what she hoped was a dazzling smile. "I feel great. Truly."

His brown eyes were soft with love and she basked in their adoration. It felt good to be loved so deeply. "Then how about we rest for a little while and see about another go-round?"

"Yes, Sir," she replied, her voice strong and sure. Seb was back and she still had his love. Inside she was beginning to feel hope fluttering in her heart and she welcomed the feeling. The only fly in the ointment was that she hadn't been completely truthful. She'd have to be eventually, of course. It wasn't something she could keep a secret forever. But tonight was only for the two of them. She would find another – better – time for that discussion.

Chapter Eleven

A MANDA CAREFULLY STROKED the mascara wand over her eyelashes as she peered into the fogged mirror in the bathroom. Pleasantly sore in a few naughty places after the passion she and Seb had shared the night before, she'd quietly slid out of bed, letting him sleep in a little longer. She had a busy day ahead but looked forward to another night with the man she'd never really stopped loving.

Seb.

The last few weeks they'd spent together had been more than she'd ever dreamed of. Each day was better than the last and the nights…

They were off the charts incredible.

"You don't need any of that, you know."

Amanda looked up into the mirror to see Seb standing behind her with a sexy grin on his handsome face.

"You may not need any help first thing in the morning but I do." She capped the mascara and tossed it in a basket on the vanity before turning around. "How did you sleep?"

"With you right next to me? Better than ever." Seb pulled her closer, sliding his arms around her and brushing her bare skin. Wearing only a bra and panties, she could feel the heat of his half-naked body against her sensitive flesh.

His lips captured hers in a kiss that seemed to sear her soul and make her weak with want. She needn't have worried though as Seb's strong arms slid under her jelly-like knees and lifted her so she was sitting on the bathroom vanity. Her legs were splayed wide as he pressed the outline of his hard cock against her already wet panties.

"That's my good girl," he crooned, lifting his mouth slightly before trailing kisses across her jaw to nibble on her ear. His questing fingers slid between her legs and under the elastic of her panties. "So wet for me, just the way you should be."

She choked as a thick digit penetrated her cunt and his thumb brushed her clit. His lips kissed and licked a path down her neck and she arched her back to give him more access, no longer able to fight the building explosion deep inside.

"Oh God," she whispered hoarsely, all thoughts of the day ahead of her gone. Right now there was only the two of them and the fiery passion that seemed to explode whenever they were together. His magic fingers tortured her as his tongue played in the valley between her breasts before dipping under the lace of her bra and licking an already hard nipple. "Seb, please."

"I like it when you say please, Mandy." His words rumbled against her skin, his breath tickling the wet flesh. At some point her hands had snuck up around his neck to tangle in his silky blond hair. He must have noticed as he pulled away, his expression stamped with passion. "You know touching me without permission isn't allowed. You know the rules."

She knew and loved them, although at times she cursed a few. As usual her mind and body reacted positively to his display of dominance, her nipples peaking under the satin of her bra.

Heart racing and flames licking at her veins, Amanda placed her hands on the vanity, her fingers gripping the edge as she fought the urge to explore his hard body.

"That's better." He smiled his approval and she felt the familiar warmth of pleasing him. "Place your hands behind you and leave them there. If you move them I won't let you come."

Knowing he would keep his word, she braced her hands behind her back, the marble vanity cold under her palms. His rough fingers found the fastener on the back of her bra and quickly squeezed it, the cool air hitting her overheated skin and the satin and lace falling away from her breasts.

"Offer them to me, Mandy." His deep, commanding voice made her shiver even as his hard cock pressed against the heat of her pussy. She arched her back until her breasts sat up high.

"Please, Sir." Her voice broke and she had to swallow hard to get the words out. He stood there motionless waiting for her to continue, his patience endless. "Please, Sir. Take me."

He grinned his acceptance and a fresh rush of cream flooded her pussy. This was what she'd longed for all those nights alone. Her heart truly belonged to this one man.

His hands cupped her breasts, the fingers pinching the tips until they were rock hard and aching. His tongue danced around the pink buds and arrows of pleasure shot straight to her pussy. He took one between his teeth and flicked his tongue at it, all the while teasing her clit until she was writhing on the counter.

When he finally lifted his head his brown eyes were almost black with passion. Pulling his fingers from her drenched pussy, he dragged her soaked panties down her legs, tossing them aside. He rubbed his hand over the fabric of his boxers before pulling them away and down. His cock sprang free, the mushroom head already flushed a reddish-purple.

She ran her tongue over her suddenly dry lips and rested her head back on the mirror. "Fuck me, Sir."

He ran a finger around her swollen clit and she moaned at the ricochet of pleasure that ran through her. He chuckled as he observed her reaction before rummaging in the vanity drawer for a condom square. In the last few weeks they'd taken to hiding them everywhere as they never knew when passion would overtake them.

He ripped at the package with his teeth and then expertly rolled it on, the latex snapping into place. Lifting her legs, he placed her feet on the counter and pressed his cock to her entrance.

His lips played with hers as he pushed inexorably farther into her pussy, taking her very breath away. She had to gasp for air as he buried himself to the hilt, sparks and fireworks already sending her close to release. Her fingers were tangled together behind her back, gripping so tight she was sure they were white from the pressure.

Everything between them had changed. Not long ago she thought she'd be alone for the rest of her life. Now she had the love of her life.

IT FELT LIKE coming home.

Being balls deep in Amanda was sublime. He'd thought he hadn't forgotten the exquisite feeling of her hot, wet cunt gripping him, but he had. Somehow his memories had dimmed over the years but they were brought back into sharp relief as he fought for control.

Pulling back, he thrust in again and then again, the pressure in his lower back building each time. They rocked together, his cock rubbing her clit with each stroke. She bucked underneath him as she neared her climax, her quickening breaths becoming more frantic. Her teeth sunk deep into her lush lower lip and she groaned as he slid over a particularly sensitive spot deep inside.

"Please, Sir. Please may I come?"

Her submission was so sweet and he struggled to be worthy of it. To be worthy of this amazing woman who made everything in his life right and good. His cock swelled even as her pussy tightened and he had to drag air into his starved lungs to be able to answer her plea.

"Yes, Mandy. Come for me now."

The words sounded hoarse and tortured but she must have heard him anyway. She whispered his name as her climax took her to the top.

She had never looked more beautiful than at this moment. Her hair had fallen from its upsweep and now was in disarray around her shoulders, the pins scattered on the marble. Her skin had taken on a rosy, flushed tone and her breasts jiggled with each stroke as she braced herself on the vanity.

He thrust one last time and finally gave in to the relentless pressure, his orgasm roaring through his balls and out his cock. Hot seed filled the condom as his dick jerked and pulsed his completion. So fucking good. If he were honest, it had never been this good with anyone else. Only Mandy.

When it was over he rested his forehead on hers, letting their breathing return to normal. Her fingers softly traced his spine and he felt her low laughter in his ear.

"Good morning, Seb."

He carefully pulled back and pressed a kiss to her adorable nose. Her smile was playful and her expression full of the same love that was squeezing his chest and making it hard to breathe.

"Good morning, Mandy. I love you."

"I love you too," she whispered. "That's quite a start to the day. Everything after this is going to seem pretty mundane."

His entire life had been that way until she'd come back into it. He couldn't imagine a day without her now and he would do everything in his power to make her happy.

"Maybe we can do it again tonight," he teased, retrieving her lingerie from where he'd tossed it.

"I don't have any other plans." She wrapped a robe around her naked body as he climbed into the shower. His inability to resist her considerable charms was going to make him late. He needed to shower up and hit the road. He had a meeting this morning and asking Chris or Dane to handle it wasn't the professional thing to do.

On the other hand…she probably needed to rinse off after their interlude.

Seb twisted on the water and waggled his eyebrows at the beautifully disheveled woman before him.

"I could use a hand washing my back."

AMANDA'S BOTTOM LOOKED too firm and perky

as she leaned over the counter, working on her list of things to do today. Dressed in a pink tracksuit, she looked completely delectable and totally fuckable. Seb couldn't stop himself from snuggling up behind her, his hands sliding around her trim waist.

How he'd managed to even get it up again this morning was a mystery. They'd made love twice last night, each time better than the last. But whenever he was near her he was as hot and horny as a teenager. He nuzzled the back of her neck so he could kiss and nip at the soft skin and smell the fresh fragrance of her just washed hair. He needed to get to the office, but one more kiss wouldn't hurt. She giggled and twisted around so his arms slid around her waist.

"You're insatiable," she scolded, but he knew she wasn't really mad—if anything she glowed with happiness. "I thought you had to go home and change so you could head to the office."

"I do," he conceded. "But I wish I could stay here and make love to you all day long. We could lounge around naked and I would feed you chocolate and champagne."

Tapping her chin, she pretended to consider his offer. He loved it when she was playful like this.

"Chocolate and champagne does sound tempting, but I have work to do today. Specifically work on your opening party. It's just around the corner, you know."

Seb didn't give a damn about that party when he had a warm bundle of woman in his arms, but she did have a point. They both had responsibilities they couldn't ignore. He had decided a long time ago that he wouldn't be one of those rich and idle trust fund babies that spent all their time partying, gambling, and traveling from one hot spot to another trying to get their picture in the gossip rags. It was one of the things that had brought him together with Amanda as she felt the same.

"I'm cooperating with that for one reason only. Mother. She's bound and determined to throw this party whether we want it or not."

"Your mother is understandably proud of you. She's so excited about this."

Seb sighed in resignation. He was embarrassed as shit whenever his mother introduced him to her friends as "My son, the decorated war hero." Now he'd have an entire evening of it. The only saving grace was that Amanda would be there by his side.

"And whatever Mother wants, Mother gets." A thought occurred to Seb and it made him smile.

"She's going to take credit for getting us back together, you know. She loves you like her own daughter."

"I love her too." Amanda placed her head on his chest and he kissed the top of her hair, luxuriating in the feel of her soft curves in his arms. "I think she did have a plan. When she offered me the job she insisted I talk to you personally."

"Crafty old woman," he laughed affectionately. "I'll have to thank her though. I don't remember the last time I was this happy, Mandy."

His feelings were reflected in her own expression. "I feel the same way but terrified too. I don't want us to screw this up again."

"We won't," he assured her. "We're older and wiser now. We know what's important."

It took all of his self-discipline not to mention the future. It was too soon to start pressuring her, but he was already thinking about marriage and a family. He'd put off being a father too long, never having felt that way about anyone else. He could even picture a little girl with Amanda's blonde hair and big blue eyes asking him to read her a story or have a tea party.

Glancing at his watch, he winced at the time. He had a nine-thirty meeting which didn't leave him much time to go home and change. "I need to go. How about dinner tonight?"

"Okay, but I'll cook since you brought food last night." They linked arms and she walked with him through the house and out of the front door.

"You don't need to go to any trouble. We can go out or order in." His mind was already starting to go into attorney mode, thinking about the day ahead.

"I'll cook," she said firmly. "Maybe even something healthy."

"Now that I want to see."

Seb's car was parked behind Amanda's in the driveway and he paused as they passed her sedan. Something didn't look quite right. A closer inspection revealed that both of the tires on the driver's side were flat. He dropped her arm and strode to the other side, kneeling down to run his hand over the expensive Pirelli.

Slashed. All four of them.

"What the hell?" Amanda was beside him, her fingers tracing the long cut in the rubber. "They were fine last night."

Seb stood and looked around in frustration. Amanda lived in an upper-middle class neighborhood, but of course that didn't mean anything these days. Crime was everywhere. Here he was supposed to be protecting the woman he loved, but instead he'd been too busy fucking her brains out while some kids trashed her tires.

Son of a bitch.

"Seb?"

Her tentative tone snagged his attention. She was frowning but not in an angry way, more questioning than anything. He took a deep breath and mustered all the control he had. Being pissed off wasn't going to solve anything.

"Sorry, I was just mad that someone did this right out here in front of your neighbors. Why don't you use your garage?"

Her nose wrinkled and she tugged nervously at her ear. "The opener is broken. I have a service coming out on Friday."

Seb pulled out his phone and dialed 911. "We'll call the police and make a report so you can give that to your insurance company. Do you have their phone number? I'll call them next."

He turned his attention to the operator as he recited the address and what had happened. When he hung up, Amanda was looking at him with a strange expression that made him pause.

"What are you doing?" she asked.

"I'm taking care of this." What did it look like he was doing?

"Seb," she said softly. "You told me not five

minutes ago you needed to go or you were going to be late. I can handle this. I'll talk to the police when they get here and I'll call my insurance company. Then I'll have the car towed to the tire place up the street." She placed her hand on his arm. "I can take care of this."

He wrestled with his conscience, wanting to do this but knowing she could handle it herself if she needed to. Once again this was about his ego, not reality. He exhaled slowly, knowing he was beat.

"I know you can, Mandy. I guess I just wanted to sweep in and save the day."

That made her smile and she reached up to take his face in her hands and kiss him softly on the lips.

"You are absolutely my knight in shining armor. But I know you have an appointment at nine-thirty and even knights can't be late. How about I'll call you when the police leave and after I talk to the insurance company, okay?"

Seb nodded in agreement, hating to run out on her when he really felt she needed him. Relationships were about being there and supporting each other, not disappearing when things got tough.

"You're still not happy, are you?" Amanda tilted her head in question, her hands on her hips.

"I want to take care of you," he finally admitted. "I want to make everything better."

"You already have." She pointed to his car. "Go to work. I'll be fine. I'll call you."

"Okay." Seb pulled open the driver's door and paused. "I know you're all grown up, Mandy, but that doesn't mean that I don't want to chase the monsters away."

"I'll make you a deal. If there's a monster I'll let you kill it."

She was teasing him now and he couldn't help but smile. "Sounds like a deal to me. I'll talk to you later. Have a good day, sweetheart. I love you."

"I love you too. Drive careful."

Seb backed out of the driveway and headed to his own home, half of his brain thinking about the day ahead and the other half still back with Amanda. He would have to get used to this new independence but he already admired her grit. She'd taken the entire incident with almost complete calm.

Now to get the day over with so he could get back to her. Now that they were together he'd never let her go.

Chapter Twelve

A MANDA SLIPPED ON her sunglasses and took a sip of water from the frosty bottle she'd pulled out of the cooler sitting beside her lounge chair. Seb had convinced her that a day at the beach would be a terrific way to get rid of some stress, so here they were. Belleair Beach was always beautiful but today seemed especially gorgeous with its sugar white sand, emerald green water, and cloudless blue sky. The only thing that could have made it better was a cool breeze. It had to be at least ninety-five degrees today with ninety percent humidity.

Relaxing under the umbrella in a brand new black bikini that Seb had brought this morning as a gift, she listened to the squawking of the seagulls scavenging for a bite to eat. There was no one feeding them today so they glided on the air currents aimlessly. She and Seb had most of the beach to themselves today as only a few residents of the small but affluent beach town were about.

Behind them were the luxury homes and condos of the rich, or at the very least the lucky. Some of the older homes may have been inherited while the newer ones went for top dollar in a market that had been hit hard a few years ago but was already coming back. Seb's friend Chris had purchased a home here as an investment and had loaned it to them for the weekend.

Amanda luxuriated in the warmth of the sun on her skin. The scent of salt air combined with the coconut aroma of her suntan lotion, the mixture bringing back memories of her youth playing on this beach with her friends. Those had been young carefree days when she hadn't had a worry in the world.

Already she was feeling more relaxed than she had in over a week. The police had found the teenagers who had slashed her tires. Just kids doing stupid stuff on a dare. They'd done the same to about a half a dozen cars in her neighborhood before the police put a stop to it. But the incident had been a turning point in her relationship with Seb. He respected her autonomy. It didn't mean he wouldn't still try to swoop in and save the day occasionally but now he knew she didn't expect it and certainly didn't need it.

What she did need was this break from her usual routine and it was even better that she was sharing it with Seb. In the last ten days she'd put together three parties in addition to his upcoming event. Plus she'd decided to sell the shelter and buy a different property and that added up to one killer of a schedule. Seb and Christian had negotiated an excellent deal with Lance Poplar and the extra money would allow them to find an even better location with more expansion possibilities. But the details of picking up and moving were exhausting.

Of course that might have more to do with the fact that she wasn't getting much sleep. She'd spent every night with Seb, and even with the best of intentions they'd end up in each other's arms making up for lost time.

"You have a very smug smile on your face, Mandy. Care to share your thoughts?"

Seb's sexy voice pulled her attention from the pristine scene before her to his handsome face. Each day they were together she fell more deeply in love with him. It made her feelings thirteen years ago seem silly and childish in comparison.

"If you must know I was thinking about you." She gave him her best coquettish smile and reached over to run her hand up his arm, the rough hair tickling her palm. He was devastatingly hunky in a pair of navy blue swim shorts that left his chest, arms, and lower legs bare. His body appeared sculpted from marble, the flesh beckoning, but this time she didn't deny herself. She let her hand glide up to his broad shoulder, massaging the tight muscles. He'd needed this day as much as she had.

"Me?" His well-shaped eyebrow quirked and his lips turned up in a smile. "You mean how I cooked dinner last night and then did the dishes?"

"That was impressive." Laughter bubbled from her lips and she let her hand trail back down his arm so their fingers could entwine. "But actually I was thinking about some of your other talents, specifically the more...intimate ones."

Her voice had dropped to a whisper but her body hummed as images of their sizzling night ran through her mind. After attaching nipple clamps to her breasts, Seb had tied her face down on the bed and worked over her bottom and thighs with a crop while a vibrator buzzed between her legs. It hadn't taken long before she'd been begging to be fucked but he'd drawn out the play, amping up her arousal. When he'd finally thrust his cock into her waiting pussy, she'd exploded almost immediately with the most intense orgasm of her life. Afterward he'd spent quite a bit of time just holding her until she'd reluctantly come back to earth.

She'd felt so close to him. He'd been in tune with her every thought and feeling, almost as if they were one person.

"I've had a smile on my face pretty much all the time as well," Seb agreed as he rubbed circles on the back of her hand with his thumb. "We certainly have chemistry to go along with the love."

Amanda knew they were lucky. Not every relationship could boast a passionate desire paired with a tender ardor. Her marriage to Emmett certainly hadn't had either of those components. Guilt that she hadn't told Seb the truth weighted heavily on her. If there was ever a moment so happy and peaceful that nothing could ruin it, it was now.

"Seb," she began tentatively, "there's been something I've wanted to talk to you about. My marriage and...everything."

"You don't owe me any explanations," Seb assured her in a soothing tone that did nothing to assuage her nerves. "We broke up and you needed to move on with your life. I understand that."

"I need to tell you. I haven't told you the whole truth about things."

Her throat tightened up as memories of her life

with Emmett came crashing back. Her fingers grasped his own a little tighter and she steeled herself for a conversation she'd rather never have.

"Whatever you tell me won't make a difference as to how I feel about you. I love you no matter what."

Amanda knew Seb loved her. She could feel it as if it was a living thing between them. But would he respect her once her story was done?

"When we called off the wedding I was devastated. I didn't get out of bed for days. Everyone was worried about me. Mother especially was concerned—" Amanda paused, not wanting to make him feel guilty but needing him to understand the depths to which she'd fallen, "I was desperate, I guess. Friends and family watched me like a hawk and eventually were able to get me up and out of the house. It was a first step back to some sort of normalcy."

She heard Seb's indrawn breath as the depth of her despair over their break up became clearer to him. It had been a mutual decision but young as she was she hadn't thought through the consequences of it.

"I'm so sorry, sweetheart." Seb said with a raw tone in his voice. "If I could go back and undo it all, you know I would. Please believe me."

Amanda did believe him. But it didn't change what had happened next, how her life had spiraled out of control.

And it had been her own damn fault.

"My parents and my friends kept dragging me out to parties and the like. Anything really to get me out of the house. I'd taken the semester off of school because I'd missed so many classes and basically I had no direction in life."

"That's when you met Emmett," he offered, his expression somber. "And you got married."

Seb made it sound so simple when in reality it had been something far different.

"I met Emmett at a cocktail party. He was handsome and charming and he seemed so easy to be around." She kept her voice under control, not allowing the past to undermine what she'd accomplished in the present. "Honestly it was because he was so different than you that I even gave him a chance. Where you were more thoughtful, he was spontaneous. Where you were intense and often brooding, he was happy go lucky. He was easy to be around so when he asked me to marry him…"

Taking a deep breath, she remembered that day clearly. Still heartbroken from their split, she'd leaped at the chance to be normal again.

"You said yes," Seb interjected. "You really

don't have to explain this, sweetheart."

"I do," she insisted. "I said yes because I still loved you so much I didn't think I would ever love anyone else, so why not marry Emmett? He said he loved me and I thought that would be enough. But it was even more than that. You don't know how many people would look at me with such pity. It was as if I was some pathetic dog whose owner dropped them off at the pound. I wanted that look to go away. So I married Emmett."

"But it wasn't enough?" he asked. "Did the looks not go away?"

He was sitting up now, his brown eyes almost black with pain he couldn't hide. She'd hurt him when she'd married Emmett. If she'd known it at the time she never would have gone through with it.

"The looks did go away but no, his love wasn't enough."

"God, Mandy." Seb shook his head, his elbows resting on his knees. "You'll never know what I went through when I found out you were engaged. Fuck, the day you got married I got rip-roaring drunk and had to be carried back to my bunk. I can't tell you how much it goddamn hurt. It hurt and the pain never completely went away. I would rather have been shot a dozen times than feel that again."

She pulled her knees up to her chest and wrapped her arms around them as if to protect herself. The rest of the story wasn't pleasant and his mention of pain brought all hers back, both mental and physical.

"I wanted to be a good wife, I really did. But Emmett knew I still loved you."

"And that hurt him?"

"No." Amanda shook her head and looked out at the water lapping gently on the sand. She pulled her sunglasses from her nose and chewed on one of the earpieces. "He never loved me so he wasn't hurt, except for maybe his pride. I think he thought that I would eventually fall in love with him, but of course that never happened."

There was a silence with only the sound of the waves and birds. "He never loved you?" Seb finally asked.

"Never. He married me for my money. He'd already gone through his own trust fund so he needed to find a rich wife. I was perfect. I was too emotionally distraught to see what game he was really playing before it was too late. He didn't tell me for a while though. It was only after we'd been married about six months that he admitted it. I think by then he knew that I was never going to fall for him."

A few nasty words fell from Seb's lips and his features had turned stone cold. If Emmett had been here with them Amanda was sure Seb would have taken a swing at her ex-husband. She would have let him.

"It doesn't matter anymore," she said hastily, not wanting this discussion to veer off track. "His avarice was the least of his bad qualities. Emmett was not a very nice person. He was especially not nice once we were behind closed doors."

Seb's eyes had narrowed and she shivered at the pure violence in his gaze. "What did he do to you? Tell me, Mandy."

Amanda took a deep breath, knowing that if Seb was this angry now what she had to tell him might possibly send him over the edge. Their idyllic day at the beach had been torn to shreds.

"The day I left Emmett was the day after he beat me so badly I had to go to the hospital."

Chapter Thirteen

THE AIR SUCKED from his lungs, Seb could barely breathe as each sentence Amanda uttered grew worse, more horrific than he'd ever imagined. All that time while he'd been in the Middle East he'd thought she was happily ensconced in marital bliss. But that hadn't been the case at all. Amanda had been trapped in a nightmare.

He hadn't been there to protect the woman he loved. He'd failed her.

Seb jumped up from the lounge chair, too angry to sit still. He wanted to find Emmett and break him in half and maybe beat on his face and ribs for a while. Even that wouldn't make up for what had happened to Amanda.

But it was a start.

She reached for his hand and tugged at it until he stood still. "Don't, Seb. I've been all through this and I've come out the other side. Sit down and let me finish." He didn't move and she pulled harder on his arm. "Please."

Sighing with frustration at the angry knot that had taken up residence in his chest, he fell reluctantly back down onto the cushion. His teeth were gritted together but for Amanda he would try and keep control.

"Go on," he urged, his gut churning with the need to beat on something or someone. Hard. "Did he hit you often?"

"Just that one time, but looking back on it now I realize he'd been working up to it from day one. He separated me from my friends and family by moving us to London. Isolated me so that I had no one to depend on but him. Verbally he was nasty to me, pounding away at my self-esteem. Typical abuser behavior. The night he hit me it really wasn't that much of a shock. I knew he hated me. He resented having to marry me for money."

Thinking of his sweet Amanda in a marriage like that was almost more than Seb could bear. She hadn't deserved any of the crap life had dealt. No wonder she was so strong and independent now, wanting to take care of even the littlest things on her own. She'd never had a man she could depend on.

Until now. Seb would make sure he was there for her every day for the rest of her life.

"The night he hurt you?" he asked, the words slightly strangled in his throat.

"I wanted to move back to Florida." Amanda shrugged as if what had set Emmett off had been meaningless. "He didn't. We fought. He hit me. The end."

"How bad?"

"A black eye. A broken arm. Two cracked ribs," she recited as if it had happened to someone else. "After being treated at the hospital the British equivalent of a social worker came to talk to me. She found me an out of the way hotel to heal in, and once I was better she drove me to the airport. Emmett, never thinking I would actually leave, hadn't tried to take my credit cards or cash. I came home and filed for divorce. He of course sued for spousal support and I paid him off. Last I heard he'd run through all the money I gave him and had to marry again. Poor woman."

"And you started volunteering at the shelter," Seb said slowly, trying to digest all that had happened in the intervening years. The fact that Amanda wasn't completely soured on men was amazing. Add in that she could still trust him to tie her up or spank her in the bedroom…it was a miracle.

To his shock, Amanda smiled and laughed. "The shelter didn't exist. I started the foundation that created the shelter. I never wanted to forget how vulnerable I felt, and I sure as hell didn't want anyone to feel the same way. I was lucky, Seb. I had the money and resources to get away. Most women don't. It only felt right that I should help them. And to be honest, it helped me too."

"The foundation and the shelter are yours?" He should have known and would have had he taken the time to look at any of the paperwork that had flowed over his desk in the last few days regarding the sale of the house to Poplin.

"Yes. I don't go out of my way to advertise the fact since I don't want the questions. Mother and Father know and my best friend Susie. That's it. Well, and now you."

"It has to be costing you a fortune." It was a stupid thing to say but Seb wasn't a man used to dealing with emotions. The fact was he didn't know what to say. He was angry and bitter and he didn't know what to do with those feelings. So much time had been wasted. So much pain. If only they hadn't been so young and foolish.

"Pretty much." Amanda laughed and reached

for his hand. "But I swear to you it's worth it when I look into the eyes of the women and children at the shelter."

Seb tugged his hand from her grasp and scraped his fingers through his hair. "How can you be so calm about this? I want to beat the ever-loving shit out of your ex-husband."

"Because I've had a long time and a lot of therapy to help me deal with it," she stated. "If I remain angry and bitter? He wins. He gets to control me from thousands of miles away and I won't let him do that anymore. I'm the one at the wheel of my life. I drive."

Amanda tapped her chest but her brows drew together in a frown. "Do you think less of me because of this? Do you want to ask me why I stayed when he started being a jerk? My parents did. Susie understood, though. She knew that I wanted to make my marriage work and that he emotionally abused me until I felt like I didn't have anywhere or anyone to go to." Her chin lifted and her blue eyes sparkled with defiance. "But maybe you're one of those people who thinks that I did something to provoke him? Or that I was an idiot to stay for so long? I've met plenty of those at the shelter, Seb. They seem to think that abuse victims ask for it in some way."

"No!" he said sharply, wanting to pull her into his arms but feeling distinctly not worthy of any of her love or admiration. "I don't think that at all. I think you must have been incredibly strong to go through all that you have."

"But?" she prompted. "I think you have more to say."

"I should have been there for you," he finally said, jumping to his feet once again. "If I hadn't been such a controlling asshole you wouldn't have called off our wedding and you wouldn't have married this loser."

"And if I hadn't been immature and self-absorbed I wouldn't have let you get away with that behavior or tried to call off the wedding in the first place." She held up her hand when he tried to speak. "What happened wasn't your fault."

"I was older," he muttered, his gaze directed at the water instead of at her. "I shouldn't have given up on us. I should have made you listen to me."

"We can't change the past, Seb. Would you rather I not have told you?" Her head was tilted to the side. "I thought we were going to be honest about everything. I'm sorry it took me so long to talk about this but I think you can see why. I thought you would lose respect for me. But that's not what happened, is it? You want to re-litigate every moment of our breakup and parcel out blame. We're past that and frankly I'm glad. We're the product of what we've been through and for that I can't be sorry. We're better people now than we were then."

Seb closed his eyes against the beauty of the day, glad that they were covered by his sunglasses. Because of one decision in their past she was forever changed.

"I put this behind me and made peace with it," she said, standing and walking to where he stood. "You have to do the same thing, Seb. Don't give Emmett any real estate in your brain. He isn't worth it."

"I need some time." He moved jerkily, his thoughts a jumble of what-ifs and should-have-beens. "Do you mind if we go?"

"No," she said carefully. "I don't, but what do you need time for? It's over and done with. It's behind us, Seb. Don't go back there."

"I have to find a way to deal with my own complicity in this. You've had time to make peace, but I've only had about fifteen minutes."

"None of this was your fault," she protested again but he didn't believe her, turning his back on her pleading expression even as images of her battered and bruised ran through his head. His stomach twisted into knots at the pictures and he had to swallow the bile that had risen in his throat.

"If I hadn't left you never would have married him."

"We both gave up on us. I only know that the past doesn't change. We have now and we have the future." Her arms wound around him from behind and she pressed her warm body to his. "I love you."

"I love you, Mandy. I just need to get my head on straight about this, that's all."

As much as he wanted to be with her, he needed the solitude to come to grips with her revelations. It was simply part of who he was and always would be. He needed the alone time to process his emotions.

And a stiff whisky or two wouldn't be bad either.

"As long as you aren't planning to pull away from me permanently, I'll give you all the time you need," she assured him softly. "I won't let your misplaced guilt affect our future."

He turned in her arms and captured her lips with his own, a solemn vow that nothing would ever separate them again. He pulled away, letting his arms drop to his sides.

"Let's gather all this stuff together and I'll take

you home."

Without speaking, they hauled their gear into Christian's house and then out to the car. Seb would take her home instead of spending the day in bed making love with her. He could only hope to God she truly understood this driving need. The minute he dropped Amanda at her house he planned to punch something and then have a drink. Not necessarily in that order. In fact, he might do both of those things more than once.

SEB SAT ON his back deck drinking a longneck and staring up at the night sky. He'd dropped Amanda at her home and come back here to think. The only problem was he was thinking that maybe he'd done something really stupid.

Always before in his adult life he'd crept away to be alone, to cogitate over a problem. Basically? To think it to death. It was his way and for the most part it had served him well. But he was beginning to wonder whether this was one of those times.

As Amanda had pointed out, the past was over. Nothing he could do would ever change it. They could only look to the present and future and try to make it the best it could be. His feelings of guilt weren't making her life better. If anything it was making it worse.

It was indulgent and selfish to act this way, and if he planned to have a life with Amanda she wasn't going to put up with behavior like that. He'd already seen the strong, independent side to her. She'd been understanding this time, but he couldn't expect that to continue.

Seb chuckled as he imagined Amanda getting in his face and telling him off. Yes, it was a very real possibility. And yet here he sat all alone feeling sorry for himself. It was no way to act, and no way to treat the woman he loved.

He needed to be worthy of Amanda and this was not the way to go about it. He'd talked about them being equals outside of the bedroom but that was all it had been. Talk. If it had been real they would be dealing with her revelations together.

Standing up and walking back into the house, Seb tossed away the half-full beer bottle into the trash. Good thing he hadn't drank much of it because he was going to get behind the wheel and drive to Amanda's house. No more separations. No more going off on his own when things got tough in some lame attempt to protect her and himself.

Life was going to have its ups and downs but

they would face them together.

"YOU LOOK A little lost, sweets."

Darby was standing at her front door with a box of chocolate cupcakes from a local bakery. She could see the fudge frosting through the clear plastic window and was surprised to find it didn't tempt her in the least. Her mind was too busy with Seb to think about eating.

"How did you know I was here?" Amanda stepped back to let Darby by. "Didn't I mention that Seb and I were going to spend the weekend at Chris's house on Belleair Beach?"

Darby slipped past her and headed straight for the kitchen. "If you did it didn't register with me. I brought cupcakes because I've barely seen you the last few weeks. If you won't come to me, I'll come to you. With chocolate."

Amanda wasn't really in the mood for Darby's brand of company tonight. She was hoping Seb would get his head out of his ass and come over, but if not she'd planned to be in bed early catching up on some much needed rest.

Darby began opening the bakery box but Amanda shook her head. "Not for me, thanks. You took a chance that I'd be home."

"I'm a gambling kind of guy, sweets." He abandoned the box of cupcakes and perched on a barstool next to the island instead. "Where is Seb tonight? I didn't see his car outside."

"Seb had a few things to do. I was planning to have an early night. It's been a busy few weeks."

She'd tried to keep the annoyance out of her voice, but from the look on Darby's face she'd hadn't quite managed it.

"And I've showed up uninvited? There was a time you wouldn't have minded, Amanda. Before Seb horned his way back into your life."

"This has nothing to do with Seb," she said defensively. Darby and Seb had never really gotten along even before but she hadn't thought much about it. Darby was far too competitive to ever be friends with another rich, handsome man.

"I can't believe you're falling for him again. Hasn't he hurt you enough? Are you just a glutton for punishment?"

"Darby." Amanda was holding onto her temper by a thread. "What happened in the past was both our fault. I'm no innocent in this. But the situation is none of your business actually. I don't remark on the women in your life – of which there are thousands. I expect the same courtesy. I told you that I expect to be treated as an adult. If you can't do that—"

"I'm trying to help you." Darby jumped up from the stool, his entire body tense and his fists tight. "How can you do this to yourself? Sebastian Gibbs is going to hurt you again, and when he does don't expect me to be around to pick up the pieces this time. I have better things to do."

The doorbell rang imperiously and Amanda sighed in resignation. She wasn't getting any peace tonight. Shaking her head at the ill-timed interruption, she pulled open the door. It was probably just her neighbor, Lois, coming by for a chat.

"Lois, it's not a good—"

"Were you expecting someone else?" Seb's voice interrupted whatever she'd been about to say. He was standing on her front porch in his well-worn jeans, red T-shirt, and abashed expression. Her heart leaped in her chest as she let her gaze lovingly run up and down his gorgeous self. She'd thought she might have to wait days to see him again but here he was.

"I thought you might be my neighbor," she explained, stepping back to let him in. "Come and say hi to Darby."

Seb entered and she shut and locked the door behind him, hoping he was here to stay. She'd deal with Darby and send him on his way.

Seb joined them in the kitchen. "Nice to see you, Darby. How are things?"

His perfectly reasonable tone didn't seem to soothe Darby's ruffled feathers.

"Actually I was just trying to talk some sense into Amanda. Since you and she have been back together, she's ceased to make any sense at all."

Sucking in a breath at Darby's caustic tone, Amanda's gaze swung to the man she loved. Seb appeared calm and controlled, simply smiling at Darby, who in comparison was red-faced.

"I'm not sure what you mean," Seb replied mildly. "Amanda is quite intelligent and practical. As for us rekindling our relationship, I don't think it's any of your business."

Seb's tone was friendly but with an edge of warning. Unfortunately, Darby didn't heed it.

"You're bad for her. You're going to break her heart again just like before. When I saw you at the party that first time I thought she'd tell you to go to hell. But you've brainwashed her. I won't let you do this, Sebastian."

"Stop it," Amanda broke in, hating the way her friend was acting. "You don't have any right to make decisions for me. I have no clue why you're even acting like this. What's gotten into you?"

Seb stepped in between her and Darby, wrapping an arm around her waist to hold her still.

"I don't like your tone. I think you need to leave now." Seb had abandoned any pretext of civility. It was clear he thought Darby was a threat both emotionally and physically.

"Amanda was a mess when you two broke up and then again when she and Emmett divorced. I'm not going to let her be hurt like that again, Seb. I won't."

Seb's muscles relaxed slightly under her palm. "Nobody is going to get hurt this time. We're in this for the long haul, Darby, and we'd like you to be happy for us. But if you can't do that I understand. But I won't back off from this. I love Amanda and I want to spend the rest of my life with her if she'll have me."

A rush of happiness almost took her breath away and her fingers tightened on his arm. Hearing the words meant everything to her.

"You're no good for each other." Darby shook his head, his jaw tight. "You'll get no blessing from me, or any of Amanda's other friends for that matter."

"I understand why you feel that way but it doesn't change anything. I'm not going anywhere unless Amanda asks me to. If she wants me to leave, I will."

Seb gazed down into her eyes with such love it made her heart ache. She wouldn't let this chance pass her by even if it meant losing a friend.

Darby peered around Seb's massive frame. "You need to choose, sweets. Seb or me. You can't have both."

Now she was really pissed off. Darby didn't treat her like a grown woman with a mind of her own. Emmitt had done the same thing. She had a knack for choosing men that didn't respect her decisions.

Until now. She'd finally got it right.

She'd been standing on her own two feet for awhile now but apparently Darby hadn't noticed. She belonged to herself, and loving Seb and wanting a future with him didn't change that.

Shaking with fury, she managed to twist around Seb's large frame. "If you're forcing me to choose then I choose Seb. You don't respect me and you don't listen to me. I'll be damned if I let another human with a dick boss me around ever again. Seb doesn't get to. You don't get to. Nobody gets to."

By the time she finished, she had stepped closer to Darby and was poking him in the chest with her index finger.

His handsome features relaxed and a smile

bloomed on his face. "Damn, you're feisty. When did that happen?"

Amanda took a deep breath and let her arm fall to her side in relief. This was the Darby she knew and loved. "I've been this way for a long time— you just didn't notice. I'm a big girl now and I can take care of myself."

His expression softened and he tucked a strand of hair behind her ear. "I liked taking care of you, sweets. You're like a sister to me. When you hurt, I hurt."

"Then when I'm happy, you can be too," she countered. "And Seb makes me very happy. Believe me, we know it won't be easy but we're not going to give up this time."

Darby's gaze traveled from Amanda to Seb and then back, his expression somber. "If he hurts you I'll kick his ass."

Laughter bubbled from her lips and she hugged the man who was like a brother to her. "You'll have to stand in line because I'll be doing it myself."

"I'm not sure how I feel about this conversation," Seb broke in dryly. "But if Darby and I can shake hands and make up I guess it's alright."

Darby's lips twisted but he stuck out his hand to Seb. "You better make her deliriously happy."

"I intend to." They shook hands although both of them didn't look too sure about this fragile truce. They hadn't been friends at the best of times. "Amanda is my number one priority."

Darby patted the box of cupcakes on the counter before turning towards the door. "I'll be keeping my eye on you, Gibbs. Now, I can see that two is company and three's a crowd, so I'll be going. I'll leave the chocolate because I have a feeling Amanda might want some later."

"Thank you, Darby." She hugged him again and pressed a chaste kiss to his cheek. "You may not believe this but having your support means a lot to me."

She would have stayed with Seb without it, but Darby seeing that she could fend for herself was an important step in their friendship. From now on they'd be on more equal footing.

"I'll call you soon." Darby strode to the open door and Amanda followed to unlock it. "I'm…happy for you, sweets, although I may not sound like it."

He tapped her on the nose before waving goodbye and climbing into his gleaming sports car. The sound of the engine dimmed as he drove away, leaving her emotionally drained. She didn't like to argue but no one was going to treat her like a child anymore.

She ran her own life and now she had the man of her dreams to live it with. He just needed to get over the guilt trip he'd sent himself on. It was time to turn their backs on the past and look firmly to the future.

"You okay, Mandy? I'm sorry about that. But I can't tell you what it meant that you were willing to give up your friendship for me. I'm humbled. Truly."

She went into his open arms and pressed her head to his chest. "It wasn't your fault. That was a conversation that had been long overdue between Darby and me. And you're the most important thing to me too. Even when you do stupid stuff like run off by yourself to feel guilty about something that wasn't your fault in the first place."

Seb's brow quirked up and a flush darkened his cheeks. "I'm guessing we need to have a talk as well."

Damn straight.

Chapter Fourteen

"**I** 'VE COME TO say I'm sorry."

Seb's hands were shoved in his jeans pockets but his soft brown eyes were full of love. Amanda crossed her arms over her chest and lifted the corner of an eyebrow.

"What are you sorry for?"

"Doing it again. Going off alone and not treating you like a partner. I promise I'll get better with practice."

She moved toward him so they were standing inches apart and placed her hands on his arms, the skin warm under her palms.

"You're already getting better. Last time took thirteen years, but this one only took about three hours and forty-five minutes. That's real improvement."

"I want to tell you it won't happen again but it might," Seb conceded with a grimace. "But I think

I can turn it around in less than thirty minutes going forward."

"We'll work on it together. You're not alone anymore."

"Neither are you." His hands came out of his pockets and he pulled her back into his arms. "I think you'll keep me on the straight and narrow, that's for sure."

She slid her arms around his middle and gazed up into his beloved face. "That's the plan, although you had me pretty worried. I thought this might take days instead of hours."

"I'm sorry I made you worry. What I did was selfish and wrong."

"Well, there is a way you can make it up to me." Amanda rubbed her cheek against Seb's broad chest.

She wanted the heaven of a quiet mind that only Seb could give her after all that had happened.

Seb pressed a kiss to the top of her head and smiled. "Anything. Name it."

"Make my mind peaceful again. Will you?"

His fingers slid into her hair and massaged the scalp, drawing a contented sigh from her lips. "I will. Poor Mandy. Your brain is going a mile a minute, isn't it? I think I have just the thing. Go into the bedroom. You know what to do."

She fled to the bedroom and stripped off her clothes before pulling the covers down on the bed. Kneeling on the rug at the foot of the mattress, she took several deep calming breaths to slow her heart rate. The problem was her quickening pulse wasn't from Darby's stunt earlier but from the thought of what Seb might or might not do to her tonight.

She waited in the quiet until finally the sound of his firm treads on the floorboard alerted her to his arrival.

"Good girl," he praised. "Let's begin."

Their rituals were so ingrained they came naturally to her now. Her body was already starting to hum as she heard him rummaging through closets and drawers but her sight was limited in the position she was in. That, she was sure, was by design.

Anticipation flared and heat curled in her belly as she felt him draw near once more.

"Stand at the foot of the bed, Mandy."

His hands helped her to her feet and she positioned herself at the end of the large four poster bed, feet flat on the floor and facing the headboard. Her hands and feet were attached to the points of the footboard with silk rope and velcro cuffs holding her in an X configuration. Her entire body was open and available, vulnerable to whatever he had planned, whatever he desired.

Amanda could feel her mind going blissfully blank, knowing she had no decisions to make. She could simply luxuriate in the feelings and sensations of the night ahead.

Seb didn't say a word either, letting the silence enfold them.

Instead he ran his rough hands all over her skin, up and down her arms, down her back, over her bottom, then up her ribcage. He paused to cup her breasts and pinch the already hard tips but then slid them down until they just brushed her pussy before rubbing her thighs, calves, and finally her ankles.

His strong fingers wrapped around the muscles and began to knead them until she was shifting her feet and groaning with pleasure. Eventually his palms slipped up to her quivering thighs and did the same there until her legs almost gave way under her. Every now and then a finger or thumb would brush her clit, and by the time he moved his hands to her ass her inner thighs were sticky with honey and she was moaning breathlessly, begging for something but not sure what.

He firmly massaged her backside and then suddenly pulled his hands away, only to have a palm come down sharply on an ass cheek. She jumped and pulled at her bonds, not really wanting to get away but loving the feeling of being helpless, completely in his dominant control.

Seb spanked her bottom until it was toasty warm before reaching down to the side of the bed and bringing back a paddle, long, thick, and covered in leather. Amanda's stomach tumbled inside of her at the thought of how that was going to feel on her already heated ass. Her fingers curled around the smooth silk of the rope and she closed her eyes as she waited for the first stroke, her pulse pounding wildly in anticipation.

When it didn't come, she peeked over at Seb who was simply standing there, watching her. He'd stripped off his shirt at some point and her gaze roamed over every muscled inch that he'd revealed. He was the epitome of a beautiful male. And he was all hers.

"Sir?"

"Just enjoying the view. You have no idea how goddamn sexy you are like this. Tied for my pleasure and submitting to my desires. It's beautiful, Mandy."

His fingers softly stroked the skin covering her spine. She shivered at the contact as it sent arrows of arousal straight to her pussy. Her nipples tightened almost painfully and she gulped air into her starved lungs.

His hand glided down her body until it lay on one generous ass cheek. He rubbed the sore flesh then removed his hand at the same time his other arm brought down the paddle.

Smack.

It landed squarely across both bottom cheeks, the impact sending her up on her toes. The heat from her ass was already traveling to her drenched pussy and clit and she gasped at the sensations that were running riot through her body.

Smack.

Smack.

Smack.

Each measured stroke found slightly different real estate than the last. Her bottom was white-hot and she was tugging on the ropes but she wouldn't have stopped him for the world.

"Do you need to use your safeword, Mandy?"

"No, Sir."

Her voice was strong and sure even as her mind buzzed and whirled at the delicious arousal that had taken control. It was as if Seb was a genius maestro playing her body in any way he wished and she was the instrument. Together they made beautiful music. How had she done without this for so long? He was the other half of her soul.

"Good girl." Amanda loved it when Seb praised her, loved the feeling knowing she was giving him exactly what he needed. "Let's try something new, shall we? I think you might like this. But first…"

She didn't know what he had planned but he wrapped a black blindfold across her eyes and fastened it tightly behind her head. Quivering with an excitement she couldn't control, a mini-orgasm skipped through her and she heard Seb chuckle in her ear. His breath was warm as he dropped a kiss on her shoulder.

"I should punish you for stealing that little one but I know you were as surprised as I was. Besides, how can I be upset when you're so responsive? Still, I think I'll make you wait a while for the next one."

The small climax hadn't taken the edge off her arousal in the least. If anything, it pushed her further toward the precipice and he'd promised to keep her there a good long time. She licked her dry lips as she heard the sound of a lighter and then the smell of vanilla begin to suffuse the air. She struggled for breath as she recognized what he had planned.

She'd never experienced it, hadn't even read about it until a few years ago. Still, the thought of

Seb dripping hot wax down her body was almost more than her heart could stand. It pounded so loudly she was sure he must be able to hear. She could hear the whoosh of blood in her ears as it was pushed rhythmically through her veins.

The darkness only made every sound more amplified. She turned her head as he moved behind her and then back as the scraping sound of a drawer being opened pulled her attention the other way.

In fact, every sense was coming stunningly alive.

The aroma of vanilla and sex filled the room. She could hear Seb's steady breaths as he moved about, and even the ropes her fingers were gripping seemed more vividly smooth.

Seb tipped her head back and took possession of her lips, his tongue demanding. It was the kiss of a man in complete control. His mouth dominated hers and she surrendered willingly, sweetly knowing her reward would be all the greater for it.

He'd barely released her lips when she felt the first heated drop of wax on her shoulder. She drew her breath in sharply and waited for pain but there wasn't any. The heat had rapidly cooled and the wax had already hardened on her skin.

Two more drops on her shoulders, the warm

liquid dripping down and tickling her sensitized flesh. Seb moved to her other shoulder, letting the wax slide down her front but never close to her nipples. He swept her hair aside and dripped the vanilla scented wax down her back, coming close to her sore ass cheeks but not quite.

His fingers rubbed the abused flesh and he placed his lips right next to her ear. "Do you want to use your safeword? It's okay if you do, sweetheart."

"No, Sir." Amanda shook her head. She wasn't sure how long her knees were going to hold out. They'd turned to water and she'd had to lock them in place to keep from falling to the floor. The room was spinning and her mind was blissfully blank as she felt the hot liquid drop first on one cheek and then the other.

Hissing at the swift pain, it quickly morphed into pleasure, her clit swollen and her pussy clenching. She wanted to beg him to fuck her but this waiting came part and parcel with submission. This was about him being in control. They would move at his pace, not hers.

A hand was at her waist, holding her firmly, and she stiffened for a moment until he murmured softly, "Relax. Lean back for me."

She knew what was coming next. Arching her

back, she sucked in a breath as wax dotted her torso here, there, and everywhere. There was a long pause and then she moaned as the fiery liquid dropped onto her hard nipple.

"Oh God!" she gasped as the other point was lavished with the same treatment, both now coated with wax. Her hips jerked and she moved restlessly, wanting and needing what he could give her but afraid of it too. She wasn't a masochist but he'd found that she liked some pain with her pleasure.

Sometimes the pain *was* the pleasure.

His hand brushed her abdomen and she could feel the glowing heat from the candle as he held it above her pussy. He waited there, giving her ample time to safeword if she wished but it was more than that. She knew what he wanted. She had to ask for it.

"Please, Sir," she whispered, purposefully relaxing all the muscles in her body, surrendering to his dominance.

She wanted to give him everything. All of herself. There was no room for questions or fear. Only trust and love.

HAD THERE EVER been a more beautiful woman in

the world than Amanda? Bound to the footboard, her face and body were flushed, her bottom even more so where Seb had paddled it and then dripped hot wax. Her nipples were rosy and pointed even under the layer of wax. Her legs were quivering, her thighs shiny with her juices. When she came her knees were going to give way and he would need to scoop her up and place her on the bed for the fucking of a lifetime.

But it was her expression that took his breath away. Her lips were curved up in a smile, the features not covered by the blindfold were in serene repose.

Her submission and trust humbled him profoundly. He'd never been with anyone like this and he knew it was because she was special. She made him more, made him want to be more for her. Just having her in his life was such a gift. He would never abuse it or take it for granted.

Seb's cock was harder than it had ever been and screaming for satisfaction, pure steel pressed against his zipper. It had been exquisite torture to take things this slowly when all he wanted to do was shove his cock in her pussy so hard and fast they would both explode, never returning to earth.

But Seb was in charge of not only this scene but his dick as well. He made the rules and that meant he might have to wait for his own release. It would be all the more intense for it.

He tilted the candle and let the pool of wax drip into her belly button, her abdomen trembling underneath his hands. Lowering it again, he spread her pussy lips with one hand while he tipped the candle ever so slightly. A small splash of wax fell on her clit and she screamed in response, her body going stiff.

Blowing out the candle, he tossed it into the glass bowl sitting on the dresser and wrapped his arms around her body as the waves of her orgasm ran through her. Holding onto her with one hand, he loosened first one wrist, then the other, her arms falling to her sides heavily. He whispered sweet, silly words into her ear until her climax finally gave up its control and she fell into his arms, a warm, soft, womanly bundle.

He unfastened her ankles and lifted her onto the bed before pulling off the blindfold. He'd have to buy her new sheets after tonight. The wax was going to make a ruin of this set but it was worth it. The image of how she'd submitted to him tonight was going to stay with him forever.

Placing her on her hands and knees, he shoved his pants down and thrust into her with one stroke. Her fingers curled into the linen and her breath came out in a hiss of satisfaction.

"Yes," she sighed.

He smacked her already sore bottom, loving the way her pussy tightened on his cock when he did.

"Yes, what?" he asked, giving her another playful slap on the other cheek.

"Yes, Sir," she breathed, struggling to her elbows, trying to get traction so she could push back when he fucked her. Already his balls were pulled up and tight and the pressure was building in his lower back.

He wanted to draw this out but it was already too much. The room was spinning and he couldn't seem to take a deep breath, his lungs starved for oxygen. He anchored his hands on her hips and rode her hard and fast. She was close to going over again and he spanked her ass a few more times knowing she liked the bite of pain, and then reached under her to pinch her nipples hard.

"Seb!" she called as her orgasm took her over once more. Her cunt muscles strangled his cock and he slammed into her one last time, letting his own climax hit him. It seemed to explode from his balls and out his cock, and he groaned as he emptied his seed deep inside of her, wanting to mark her as his woman forever. Their mating had been that harsh and primitive in its way but he would hold her tenderly when it was done.

Eventually they collapsed together on the bed, a tangle of arms, legs, and messy, waxed-smeared sheets. Seb pulled her close and stroked her hair and back, letting the peaceful silence penetrate their soul.

Except that there was something he wanted to say, and suddenly the urge was overwhelming. He needed to know if she felt as deeply about their future as he did.

"I'll be right back, sweetheart." Seb dropped a kiss on her cute nose and headed into the bathroom. He came back out with a warm washcloth and some lotion and very carefully used it to remove the wax before wiping down her skin, thankful that he'd laid in a supply of things both for their dominant-submissive scenes and the aftercare. When he was done he propped up all the pillows against the headboard and beckoned for her to join him.

"I love you, Mandy. Do you love me?"

She looked up at him then, her blue eyes almost violet with emotion. "Do you really need to ask? I love you more than anything. What do you think all this has been about?"

She was giggling at him and he didn't blame

her. Perhaps in thirty or forty years he would get used to being this happy. He leaned over to dig something out of his pocket and held it up.

"Enough to spend eternity with me?"

Her eyes widened at the small, light blue velvet box in his hand. He grinned as he flipped it open, the diamond winking in the lamplight.

"Oh, Seb." Amanda's eyes filled with tears. "I never thought we'd get a second chance." She peered down at the ring and frowned. "Wait, this is a different ring. I gave my ring back to you, remember?"

"Vividly, even though I insisted I wanted you to keep it. I still have it but I thought since this was a new start, as different people, you should get a new ring. You can sell the other to help fund the foundation if you like. Or we can throw it in the Gulf of Mexico. It's up to you."

She held out her left hand and he slid the ring on her finger, then pressed a kiss to the knuckle.

"It fits perfectly," she exclaimed. "It's beautiful, Seb."

"So what do you think? Eternity sound good?"

Amanda shook her head but a smile played on her lips. "It won't be nearly long enough. What's more than an eternity?"

Seb pulled her into his arms, knowing there

would be many days and nights like this to come. It almost hadn't happened and he probably had his mother to thank that it had. She'd make sure he never forgot it too.

"I have no idea, but for you I will find out."

He'd do anything for her, but he already had the one thing he'd always wanted. Mandy.

Epilogue

I T WAS THE night of the firm opening party and Seb's home was full of people, some of which he knew and a hell of a lot which he didn't. He could only assume they were friends of his mother and father or perhaps Chris or Dane's parents. Either way, looking for the woman he loved was like looking for a needle in a haystack. Amanda was nowhere to be found.

"You're supposed to be mingling." Chris slapped Seb on the shoulder with a grin and elbowed Dane in the ribs. "We're supposed to be celebrating and making contacts tonight."

Seb scanned the crowd of local fat cats and hanger-ons. Only a small portion of these people could be called real friends. The kind of law firm they wanted wasn't going to take on the case of a politician caught with his hand in the cookie jar or a corporation selling dangerous products to save a few pennies. They'd already decided that their firm would be about the working men and women who weren't being given a fair shake in today's society. Seb and his friends had been born with much and wanted to give back.

"I doubt any of these people will be looking to hire us when they find out what kind of cases we've already taken," Seb said dryly. "Besides, I'm looking for Amanda. Have you seen her?"

"I saw her talking to the caterer out back of the house," Chris offered. "Just a few minutes ago as a matter of fact. Aren't Dane and I good enough to talk to?"

"Actually, I do have something to talk to you about. I asked Amanda to marry me over the weekend and she said yes."

Dane and Chris both slapped Seb on the back and gave him their congratulations, although Dane looked slightly shell-shocked.

"We've decided that we're not going to let the past get in the way of a damn good party so we're planning a big wedding. That brings me to the whole best man and groomsman thing. Shit, I want both of you as my best man."

Dane threw back his head and laughed. "Clearly, I'm the best man of all three of us but weddings and commitment make me itch. I'm happy to step aside and let Christian grab the honor."

"Are you sure? I'm okay either way," Chris argued. "If I'm best man at Seb's wedding, then you can be best man at my wedding, and Seb can be best man at your wedding. That would be fair."

"Whoa, slow down." Dane held up his hands and let out a whistle. "There isn't going to be any wedding for me, so you can be best man for Seb and he can return the favor. Leave me out of all this nuptial bliss, for fuck's sake."

Seb chuckled at the affronted expression on Dane's face. The man had a strange idea about women and money that neither Seb nor Chris had been able to shake. Dane's only hope was a female that would prove to him that there were good women out there.

"Fine," Seb agreed before turning to Chris. "Susie is going to be Amanda's maid of honor so you'll be paired with her for much of the festivities before and during. Will you be okay with that?"

Dane groaned and rolled his eyes. "Better you than me, man. That girl doesn't know when to give up. She's been dogging my heels for years."

"You are a self-centered prick," Chris pointed to Dane. "Susie's a good kid with obviously poor taste in men if she's after you."

"Kid is a good word for Susie," Dane replied.

"She's ten years too young. Besides, she's not my type."

"Her IQ is much higher than most of the women you date," Chris agreed.

"It's not her brains." Dane hesitated for a moment and then shrugged carelessly. "Physically she's not my type."

"You mean she's not stick thin?" Chris asked, his lips pressed together.

"You said it, not me," Dane denied, shaking his head vigorously. "I just said she's not my type."

"Fuck, don't let Amanda hear you say that. She'll kick you in the balls," Chris declared. "Sometimes you can be a real shit, Dane. Let's just drop the whole damn subject. I think I'm man enough to keep Susie company for a few days without whining."

Seb watched the exchange between Dane and Christian with interest. Chris was always easy-going and willing to help out so his attitude about spending a few days with Susie wasn't a surprise, but his hard-ass attitude with Dane was unusual.

"Did you tell them about the wedding?"

Amanda had joined them, linking her arm with Seb's. "I did. Chris is going to be the best man and Dane one of the groomsmen. How did Susie take the news?"

"She's excited." Amanda's smiled and squeezed his hand. "We've already got a date to go dress shopping."

Dane shook his head and headed for the bar. "I need another drink if all you're going to talk about is wedding shit from now on."

Amanda's eyebrows shot up at Dane's hasty departure. "Wow, is he okay? I promise to keep the wedding talk to a minimum if it bothers him that much."

"Talk about it as much as you want," Seb growled, already tired of Dane's shit. "He's got the usual bug up his ass that we all simply ignore."

"I'll deal with him." Chris tossed back the remainder of his beer. "I think it's time for him and me to have a chat about not being the center of the fucking universe."

Seb and Amanda watched as Chris strode after Dane, his features set with purpose. Seb didn't envy Dane right now. Chris rarely lost his temper but something told Seb that today was going to be the exception.

"Never a dull moment with you three," Amanda chuckled, looking up at him from under her lashes. "I can't wait for the party to be over so we can be alone. I believe we have a date to make love under the stars."

Seb looked down into the melting blue eyes of the woman he loved. "Later," he promised. He couldn't wait until this party was over and everyone was gone. He wanted to be alone with Amanda.

"Later," she agreed.

After all, they had forever.

The End

I hope you enjoyed Seb and Amanda's second chance love story! Continue the journey with Christian and Susie...
Diamonds and Revolvers

Christian wants Susie, but Susie wants Dane.

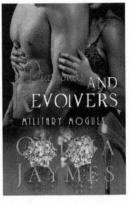

While on leave five years ago, Christian Rhodes spent one amazing evening with Susie Langtree. He didn't even kiss her but a man knows when a woman is special. So he's thrilled they'll be thrown together at Seb and Amanda's destination wedding.

Susie has been pining after Dane Braxton for years and this wedding is her chance to make him see all that he's been missing. She's packed her high heels and sexy lingerie. He won't know what hit him.

Quickly sizing up the situation, Chris realizes he has to move fast and show her the time of her life. Swept off her feet by flowers and candlelight, Susie is seeing Chris in a whole new light.

Everything is going great, until Dane makes a move on Susie...

About the Author

Olivia Jaymes is a wife, mother, lover of sexy romance, and caffeine addict. She lives with her husband and son in central Florida and spends her days with handsome alpha males and spunky heroines.

She is currently working on a series of full-length novels called The Cowboy Justice Association. It's a contemporary romance series about lawmen in southern Montana who work to keep the peace but can't seem to find it in their own lives in addition to the erotic romance novella series – Military Moguls.

Visit Olivia Jaymes at:
www.OliviaJaymes.com

Cowboy Justice Association

Cowboy Command

Justice Healed

Cowboy Truth

Cowboy Famous

Cowboy Cool

Imperfect Justice

The Deputies

Military Moguls

Champagne and Bullets

Diamonds and Revolvers

Caviar and Covert Ops

Emeralds, Rubies, and Camouflage

Made in the USA
San Bernardino, CA
01 December 2015